Summer

at

The Point

By: Kelly Traylor

Summer at The Point

Summer At The Point by Kelly Traylor

© 2009 Kelly Traylor

ISBN: 978-0-578-01367-1

Published by Lulu Publishing, Inc.

Printed in the United States of America.

Imagination is an incredible gift and one should always
live out the life they imagine.

Summer at The Point

Mom and Dad I just want to thank you for always believing in me and for teaching me focus and determination. Brittany, I love you, I could not ask for a better sister. To Barbara, you have offered me so much and I know that I can always count on your support. Shannon, I am grateful for all of the priceless memories.

Summer at The Point

Foreword

Skyler Richardson was a small-town girl with big city dreams. Allie was a nursing student working to pay off college loans. They met at Rock Springs Country Club and Resort where Allie was working as temporary summer help and Skyler was enjoying her last summer before starting college. Skyler's family owned a share of the resort and they are known for being one of the wealthiest families in the area. Despite her deep pockets and high social status, Skyler was very conservative with her money and did not see any reason for acting as if she was better than anyone else was. She was nineteen and after taking the last year off to travel with her mother, Skyler's dad had the rest of her future mapped out. Skyler was to follow her father's example and attend a prestigious university in North Carolina and upon graduating; she would attend law school and eventually become a partner at the law firm her grandfather founded over fifty years ago. However, Skyler had other plans in mind, she wanted to sing and create her own path. Skyler was a free spirit and she did not do well with plans. Allie and Skyler met just as the summer was starting and instantly they became friends. Memorial Day weekend meant not only the members being back for the start of their summer long vacation but they had brought friends and extended family along with them as well. Allie knew she was in for a summer that would be full of stress, excitement, and hopefully the start of a new beginning.

CHAPTER ONE

It was one fifteen in the morning and the bartender announced last call. Allie's feet were killing her so she headed into the back room to start cleaning up after a long night of dinner, drinks, and drama. She knew that if she could straighten up her server station, by one thirty she could call it a night. It took Allie only a second to realize that she was not alone in that back room. As Allie opened the door of the liquor cabinet, a disheveled brunette with a short stylish hairstyle and a sporty shape, came barreling out followed by a younger male with unkempt curls and baggy jeans. The girl was Skyler Richardson and the boy was Braxton Davis the restaurant manager's son. After some strange looks and an awkward silence, Braxton managed to

Summer at The Point

introduce himself, and Skyler did the same.

"You're Allie, right?" Skyler asked with a little hesitation.

"Yes, I am. But..." Allie was a little baffled.

Skyler stopped her short to say, "Alex told me about you. So what exactly is your job again?"

"Most nights I'll be here as a server, but I'll be working at the coffee shop some too. Who's Alex?" Allie did not know any of the staff here yet and wondered how people already knew her.

"You and I should hang out? Any plans for after work?" Skyler responded ignoring Allie's questions.

"Well, no but..." Allie could not think of an excuse quick enough. It was not that she did not want to hang out; Allie was just worn out from a busy shift and she still had some unpacking to do.

"Good, I'll be out front waiting. Just keep the closet incidence between the three of us. Okay?" Skyler left the room just as quick and boisterous as she had entered.

Allie could not understand why out of all the people at the resort, Skyler would chose to hang out with her. Maybe this is what she needed, a way to take her mind off the life she left behind in her college town. Allie was just getting out of a three-year relationship and she was dying to meet new people, even though the idea of awkward silence in new social situations made her nauseated. Allie knew that she needed to put herself out there.

Allie finished her cleaning and shrugged her shoulder's as she flicked off the light. "What do I have to lose?" She said to herself as she locked the back room and headed out the front door.

When Allie first got out to the parking lot, she did not see Skyler. She briefly looked around and then heard a yelp coming from behind the large oak tree to the right of the restaurant. Allie threw up a hand to wave back; it was Skyler and Braxton along with another young guy that she did not recognize. They were sitting in a golf cart that Allie assumed belonged to Skyler's family. Allie made her way across the lot to greet her new friends. She threw here tie-dyed bag on the seat as Skyler introduced her to the unfamiliar face sitting on the back seat of the cart.

"Allie, this is Alex Shea, he's worked here for the past three summers. He is one of the locals who commute to work. He is the one who told me your name. His cousin works at the main office; she knows the scoop on all of the new employees." Skyler proceeded to tell Allie about all of the gossip Alex's sister hears and some of the popular rumors that are already taking effect this summer. "I can't wait to hear what will be said about me this summer. I'm always a main topic around here, but this summer I plan to live it up and really give these stiffs something to talk about." Skyler seemed to be generating some kind of scheme as she confessed to them her desire to break free from her family's strict rules.

Skyler started the golf cart and began to give Allie a tour of the grounds. Allie wondered what the deal was with this Alex person. He did not even look at her or show any sort of acknowledgement when she sat next to him.

Skyler took off only to stop suddenly after driving to the bottom of the hill behind the restaurant. "Switch seats with Allie, Braxton so she can get the best view of what I'm trying to show her." Skyler nudged Braxton off the golf cart to make room for Allie.

Braxton jumped on the back and playfully put his arm around Alex saying, "Guess you're my date for tonight man."

Finally, Alex showed that he could speak as he laughed back saying, "Don't fall in love with me now, I'm not looking for a commitment."

"Okay children, just hang on. I swear I can't take you two anywhere." Skyler hoped Allie appreciated the humor.

They rode through the winding golf course and around the coastline of the lake as Skyler pointed out the hot spots, the "important" people's condominiums, the tennis courts, coffee shop, and small shopping center.

Summer at The Point

Skyler did not stop the golf cart until she arrived at her family's condominium. She wanted Allie to have some insight as to why she was so adamant about rebelling against her parents.

"They're still up. Drinking with the Carmichael's I'm sure." Skyler let out a deep sigh before continuing. "I don't know how they do it; always keeping up this front of a happy family. As soon as the summer is over mom heads back to Plymouth and dad back to Pittsburgh as always. It is only in the summer that we are a family. That is why this summer; I am going to let them know that I have had enough. I am out of the house now and I can finally use the money they have been adding to my savings since I was a child. I barely know you Allie, but I am going to ask for your help. I need to have fun this summer and gain the courage and confidence I need to let my family know that I will not be following their plan for me. Braxton, Alex, I know you will support me; you have since we met. Let's really live it up this summer."

After taking in what Skyler had just said, Allie was able to address something that had been nagging at her. "So after the summer, what do you plan to do?"

Skyler shook her head and said, "That's the beauty of it, I'll be able to do whatever I want. Even though now I don't know, by the end of summer I'm confident I will."

"Fair enough." Allie replied. "I have to admit a summer of living it up with no rules and no plans sounds a lot better than following a schedule and meeting expectations. My hours aren't bad, but I'm not sure how much I'll be able to enjoy myself this summer." Allie regretted taking a second job. She was supposed to have only one job as a server, but when the barista role at the coffee shop came available, she jumped at the chance for extra cash.

"Don't worry about it. We can get you the schedule you need." Braxton stated. "I can make sure you have most Saturday nights off. Tips are no good on Saturday night because of the second floor buffet and all the parties around the resort. I'll take care of it, my dad has me type up the schedules."

"Nice. So there we have it. It's the four of us this summer." Skyler took the boys back to Braxton's cabin. Alex stayed with him on the night's he worked. The boys said their goodnights to Skyler and Allie promising that tomorrow night would be more exciting.

Skyler headed towards the back of the grounds to take Allie to the living quarters the resort had set up for their summer employees. Most of the lights were still on and you could see that the once divided boys and girls cabins had already merged. Allie was dreading what she would stumble upon once she entered the cabin. She had not had a chance to befriend any fellow employees. Since she arrived late yesterday, Allie planned to make her way to her room without acknowledging anyone. Since she worked all day, she did not feel like socializing. Allie just wanted to go to bed.

"Thanks for the tour and the company tonight. Your friends are nice. Um, I guess I'll see you around." Saying goodbye was awkward. Allie did not know if Skyler was really planning to hang out with her this summer like she had implied, or if she was just going to stick with the rest of the members.

"How about we do this again tomorrow? What time do you get off?" Skyler asked. "I'm supposed to hang out with Braxton and I could use another girl around."

"Okay. I get off after dinner rush tomorrow since I closed tonight. I should be finished by ten." Allie had to admit that she did enjoy talking to Skyler and hoped they would continue to be friends. It was nice to have a friend who did not already know her past and judge her for it.

"Great. See you tomorrow then." Skyler remarked as she sped away and headed back towards her condominium.

Allie held tight to her tie-dyed bag as she crossed the yard in front of the cabins where sunburned college students were still excited about their summer jobs and the connections they were making. She was about to turn the knob to her room when someone behind her said, "So you know Skyler Richardson?"

Allie turned to see who this person was that followed

Summer at The Point

her to her room only to ask about Skyler. It was a dark haired, brown eyed, male sporting a cowboy hat, glasses, and a big grin. "I'm Billy by the way. Billy Douglas, I manage the second floor buffet at the restaurant. I just wanted to know about Skyler, does she have a boyfriend?"

"Skyler, um well, I met her tonight actually." Allie explained.

"Oh, well what do you think about her?" Billy asked.

Allie was annoyed at his persistence, but she told him what she thought he wanted to hear. "She is a cool girl, not stuck up like the rest of these snobby rich girls. I do not think she has a boyfriend, but she hangs tight with Braxton Davis. I could talk to her for you if you want. I am meeting up with her and Braxton tomorrow after my shift." Allie did not know if perhaps she said a little too much about Skyler, but Billy seemed like an okay person.

"Thanks. That would be really cool of you." Billy replied.

"No problem. Oh, I'm Allie by the way, waitress, first summer here." Allie offered her hand to Billy as she introduced herself.

"Nice to meet you. I apologize for being rude, I should have allowed time for a proper introduction before I started asking so many questions." Billy apologized.

"Oh, don't worry about it. I didn't even pay it any

14

mind." Allie lied politely.

"It's my second summer here. Last summer I could not even get the courage to talk to anyone about Skyler. I felt like I had to do something this year. I appreciate it. Sorry to bother you." Billy said goodnight and walked back toward the crowd of employees that was finally dwindling down and perhaps about to call it a night.

Allie finally made it to her bed and within minutes, she was asleep.

She woke to the sound of screaming lifeguards and caddies who had overslept and were rushing to get ready for another day of work.

CHAPTER TWO

"What the heck!" Allie said with frustration in her tired voice as she heard a hair dryer fire up.

"Good afternoon. Sorry, I'm just getting back from my shift, didn't mean to wake you." The voice came from the bathroom that joined two double rooms. "I didn't get a chance to meet you yesterday, I'm DJ. I'm a life guard." DJ stuck her head out from behind the door and continued. "My shift starts at six and I get off at twelve. I only work four days a week, so what do you do? What is your schedule like?"

Allie could not help but wonder if DJ had even taken a breath while spitting out all that she said. She was obviously a morning person. Allie looked up to see the smiling face of a girl whose braces gave her the appearance of being slightly younger than Allie. However, her tanned skin and blonde hair would definitely attract the male employees no matter what her age. "I'm Allie. I am a waitress and barista. I don't know my official schedule yet. It is still in progress. I go in at four today and I'm off hopefully by ten." Allie just gave her what she asked and figured they could get better acquainted later. Right now, she wanted to lie in bed until she absolutely had to get up. "I'm going to crash for a little bit longer. I'm not trying to be rude, I'm just sleepy." She offered this explanation to DJ before rolling back over and attempting to go back to sleep.

"No problem, I'm on the way out anyway. See you later." DJ tied her hair up in a ponytail, grabbed her bag and headed out the door.

Allie wondered where DJ was off to in such a hurry. Then she turned and looked at the clock. It was already one-thirty in the afternoon. Allie thought about all the things she could be doing and decided to get up. "It's already Sunday, just one more day of this long holiday weekend." She offered this reminder to herself as encouragement to get a shower and get on with the day.

Allie was about to step into the shower when she heard voices from the room that adjoins hers. "Oh wow, have you seen Skyler yet? I heard she has been running around with some of the employees and Mr. Davis' son Braxton. How cute is he this summer? It's amazing how much a guy can change in just a year." Allie could

17

hear the girls laughing. "I might have to put hanging out with him on my summer to do list."

"You've got that right. He is pretty attractive, but still not as cute to me as Alex." A rather mousey second voice chimed in.

"It's always about Alex with you. Well, I guess this means Skyler is over Bobby. Maybe that means he's fair game. I'll have to check into that." This snobby voice had to belong to one of the members but Allie wondered why they were in an employee's room. There was a certain sarcasm and mischief in her voice. She came off as if she saw herself as being better than Skyler. She wondered why they cared so much who Skyler was seeing. Allie wondered if this girl was perhaps Alex's girlfriend. Allie did not want to hear any more. She got in the shower and thought that she could find out a little more about this Bobby character from others, before bringing this to Skyler's attention.

Allie turned on the water and tried to clear her mind.

"Hey, open up!" A girl shouted from outside the bathroom door. Allie ended her shower a little sooner than she would have liked. She wrapped a towel around herself and cracked open the door.

"Did you need something?" Allie asked as she answered the knocking of a rather angry girl.

The short, chubby brown-haired person just glared

back at Allie as if she was supposed to read her mind. Instead of verbally responding, she held up a red flag and a piece of white stationary with words written in all caps.

Allie grabbed the letter to take a closer look. Still not knowing what this girl expected from her.

HEY SUCKER! YOU HAVE BEEN RAIDED!

Those few words had this girl extremely upset. Allie offered a shrug of her shoulders before handing the paper back to her.

"Well, do you know anything about this? I thought since you were here, that maybe you knew. What should I do? I don't know what they took." The girl panicked.

"I'd stay calm and wait to see if you can find what they took. I am sure that it is just a stupid prank being pulled on new employees. They are probably just trying to get a rise out of you." Allie did not tell the girl that she overheard someone in her room earlier. She thought she might need to wait and identify the girl that she heard before she started pointing fingers.

Later, just to be safe, after Allie got dressed she locked everything with any sort of value in the trunk she brought from home. Then, she slid it under the bed where it fit perfectly. If someone wanted to steal her things, they would have to work for it.

It was now three o'clock and Allie had just enough time

Summer at The Point

to grab some lunch before heading into work. She threw a change of clothes, a magazine, and some cash into her bag then walked toward the coffee shop for a quick bite to eat. When she arrived, she saw a familiar face at the tall table in the corner. Alex was sitting alone but he definitely had the attention of a table of teenage girls who were giggling and smiling in his direction. Allie decided to head over to him. "Mind if a join you?" He nodded and pointed as if to invite her to sit down. "You don't say much do you?" Allie could hear the girls questioning each other about who she might be and one girl in particular seemed to be rather annoyed by Allie's presence.

"Yeah I guess I can be just a little slow to open up. Before long you'll be begging me to keep quiet." He looked up briefly and winked as the server came to take Allie's lunch order.

"Grilled cheese and water to go. Thanks" Allie looked back at Alex and this time she really looked at him as his eyes peeked over the rim of his soda.

"What?" He asked, confused by the look Allie was giving him.

"How old are you? If you don't mind me asking." Allie was noticing a certain innocence in Alex's eyes. Allie began to notice Alex and how incredibly different he was from other guys she had known. He's was cute too, in a way that normally would not catch Allie's eye. However, something about Alex intrigued her.

"Seventeen. I'll be eighteen at the end of the summer." Alex made eye contact with Allie this time. "Too young, right?"

"Well, um, I don't know. Too young for what?" Allie acted as if she did not know he was trying to see if she was into him. "I don't pay attention to age. I just enjoy being around cool people. I figured if you were one of Skyler's friends then I needed to get to know you better." Allie did the math in her head. There was a three-year difference between the two of them since Allie had just celebrated her twentieth birthday.

"Are you hanging out with Skyler tonight?" Alex asked.

"Yeah, I should be off by ten tonight. So I told her that I would meet her after." Allie replied.

"Braxton's going to be with her too I'm sure. Guess that means I will be too. We should all go out to The Point tonight." He winked again as he got up from the table, which showed even though he was only seventeen; he was no amateur when it came to flirting.

"Time to get to work. I'll see you later." He smiled as he turned to leave paying no mind to the table of young girls calling out to him.

Allie managed to get out a "bye" as she grabbed her food, paid her bill and gathered her things to head off to work. She wondered about The Point that Alex had mentioned. She did not remember hearing any mention of it when Skyler was giving her the tour. Allie was curious. Allie would question Skyler about that tonight.

CHAPTER THREE

It was nearly ten thirty and Allie figured Skyler had given up on her so she clocked out and headed out the front door. The sound of an old bicycle horn made Allie jump as she stepped out into the parking lot. It was Skyler, alone on her golf cart. Allie made her way over to the Skyler and asked, "Where are the guys."

"They're still working." Skyler sat the bicycle horn down on the seat. "They will be off at eleven and they are going to meet us at The Point. Heard you and Alex talked over lunch today?" Skyler raised an eyebrow and looked Allie's way.

"I was just being friendly. I didn't recognize anyone at the coffee shop so I sat with him." Allie could tell Skyler had heard something more from the rumor mill but Allie was not concerned. "By the way, do you know of any room raiding pranks that I should be aware of?"

23

"Oh, Veronica must be back to her old tricks. She always steals from the employees. She used to work here. Well, that is until her mom married my uncle and now she is one of the most obnoxious member girls here. Another reason I don't hang around that crowd." It was obvious that Skyler did not care for her cousin at all. Once Skyler offered an explanation, Allie felt certain Veronica was the one who broke into her neighbors' room. "She never takes anything valuable though, so don't worry about that. She just likes to stir stuff up. Did she get into your room?"

"No, it was the room next door to mine. I overheard her talking though, I was in the shower at the time." Allie explained.

Since they had a little time to kill, Skyler took Allie back to the cabin to change instead of using the bathhouse, which was the original plan.

The girls jumped off the golf cart and ran inside. Allie decided to put on one of her cuter outfits. She also touched up her make-up and let down her hair. Allie was acting as if she was excited to see someone, maybe she was.

"So who is Bobby?" Allie asked as she applied some eyeliner.

"How did you hear about him?" Skyler's voice took on a lower tone as she questioned Allie.

"The girls that were in my neighbor's room were talking about him and Alex too. They said you used to date Bobby?" Allie hoped Skyler would not take offense to her asking about her personal life. "You don't have to tell me if you don't want."

"I guess Marcy was with Veronica this time. She is obsessed with Alex. Anyway, I don't mind talking about Bobby." Skyler tossed a candy wrapper into the trashcan. "Bobby Dixon was my off-and-on boyfriend for the past two years. We broke up just before the start of this summer. He is Alex's brother, but they are not anything alike. I guess you could say he is a 'bad boy.' I'm not saying that I'm no longer interested. It is just that I feel like I need something and someone new. That is why I am hanging out with Braxton this summer, because with him there is no pressure. I love the adventure and the uncertainty. I love that everyone is talking about us and asking what we see in each other. I love this summer fling, if that is even what this is, and I'm living it up."

"So if he's Alex's brother, does that mean he works here or is he a member?" Allie was realizing that it is going to be tough to remember everything she is learning from Skyler.

"Neither. Well, he used to work here, but he got into some trouble. Now he just comes as a guest of some of the male members. Like I said, he is nothing like Alex." Skyler was adamant about making it certain to Allie that Bobby and Alex were nothing alike. "He lives with

Summer at The Point

his mother in the city. Bobby has a couple of tattoos, one on each arm and another in the center of his back. He also has his eyebrow pierced. He's pretty laid back most of the time, but he can get also get pretty intense." Skyler was looking down the entire time she was speaking about Bobby. "Then again, he knows just what to say to make any girl smile. Even when I was mad at him, all he had to do was compliment me and give me that mischievous grin and I forgot what I was mad about. He made me feel beautiful." Skyler turned to glare out the window. "Then he cheated on me while I was in France with my mother and I was done." Skyler let out a big sigh. "The end."

"Wow. I'm sorry." Allie did not know what else to say. She tried to get a picture in her head of Skyler with someone like this but it just did not seem to form. "Any regrets?"

"I can't say that I regret any of the time I spent with Bobby. He is a lot like Braxton in a way. I was never a very confident girl and I can be shy when it comes to relationships. I think Bobby helped me to feel good about myself and learn to open up and Braxton is helping me to stay that way. I was jaded by Bobby's smooth personality and at first, I didn't notice his darker side. But, I think that everything happened for a reason. Braxton has most of Bobby's good characteristics and none of his bad ones. I can honestly say that I'm happy right now." Skyler had a grin on her face now as she thought about seeing Braxton later. "I'm not after love this summer. This girl just wants to have fun." Skyler added.

Allie switched off the bathroom light and closed the door behind her. "I'm glad everything is working out for you. Now let's go live it up! The night is young." Allie offered a hand to Skyler to pull her up off the bed. "So what is The Point?" Allie asked Skyler as they headed out the door and back outside to the golf cart.

"It's a little spot down by the lake behind the coffee shop. There is an old gate back there to keep people away, but it doesn't stop anyone. It does not look like much of anything in the daytime, but at night, it is our own little getaway." Skyler's description painted a visual in Allie's mind. "You did remember to put your bathing suit on under your clothes, right?" Skyler loved The Point. It was her favorite place on the entire resort, and it included, a small beach area behind a big oak tree and some large rocks that made the best lounge chairs.

"Yeah I have it on." Allie was not expecting to get in but she had worn her suit just in case.

Allie glanced at her watch. It was now 11:30, which meant that Braxton and Alex should already be off and perhaps they were already at The Point waiting.

Skyler parked the golf cart to the left of the coffee shop so it could not be seen from the normal path. There were already three other golf carts back there and Allie could see at least ten people scattered on some large rocks behind the gate that Skyler had mentioned. It only took a second for Allie to notice Alex standing shirtless on the rocks with a baseball cap turned to the side, he was showing off some dance moves and trying to get a laugh out of a group of younger girls.

"Hey boy, who taught you to move like that?" Skyler shouted as she walked briskly towards the crowd. "Come on girl!" She screamed back toward Allie.

Allie took at deep breath and convinced herself that she was going to have a good time.

CHAPTER FOUR

"Ladies, ladies, ladies!" Braxton was trying to explain something to the group, but he stopped himself short to turn his attention to Skyler. "There's my girl!" He grabbed Skyler's hand and pulled her up onto one of the big rocks. "Excuse me friends, I have some business to attend to." It was obvious Braxton loved drawing attention to his "relationship" with Skyler. He also did not mind being a little over-dramatic so he dipped her over his knee and kissed her.

Skyler looked around and saw two girls whispering and pointing in her direction. She grins at the thought of the rumors spreading. She knew that what she had with Braxton was not serious, so she shrugged her shoulders and continued with the act.

"Well, I guess the secret's out my love." Skyler and Braxton laughed at the idea of love. They have been friends for years and the flirtation continued to get more intense as each summer came and went.

"Don't be so quiet over there missy, come meet everyone!" Braxton addressed Allie this time. Braxton mentioned a name for every face, but there was no way Allie could remember all of them just yet.

Allie did notice one girl that looked familiar. She appeared to be about seventeen, her streaked hair was wet and knotted on the top of her head, and she began to glare back at Allie once she realized where they had seen each other before. Allie managed a "hey" and remembered getting that same dirty glare at the coffee shop from the same girl after she sat down with Alex.

"Ready for a swim?" Braxton threw his arms up as he asked this question to everyone.

Allie was not quite ready to get in so she took a seat on one of the rocks once everyone jumped in. She watched them having fun in the water and in her mind she was trying to remember who everyone was. Then she noticed Alex was not in the water. She saw him earlier, but where did he go and why did she care.

"Getting in?" A voice came from behind Allie making her jump. "The water feels great, they'll be in for a while you might as well join them." Alex climbed up the rocks to sit next to Allie.

"I'm not quite ready to jump in. Thought I'd sit here for a few minutes first?" Allie's stomach began to knot up around Alex, but she could not understand why.

"Want some company while you sit, or should I go on and jump in with the rest of them?" Alex grinned and turned to face Allie.

"Company would be great, but I don't want to ruin your fun." Allie had to grin back when she saw that he had dimples that made him resemble a young Leonardo.

"So what's your story?" Alex asked.

"Ha. Well, I don't have too much to say." Allie responded.

"I'm sure there's a story. Come on, you have to keep me entertained." Alex joked.

Allie was not sure how much Alex really wanted to know, so she figured she would just hit the highlights. "I took this job to escape from my college life. I just finished my second year. I was planning on spending my summer at home, but then I heard they were hiring here so here I am. I told you it wasn't much of a story." Allie was starting to feel more comfortable.

"Okay. What are you majoring in?" Alex asked.

Summer at The Point

"Nursing, not sure if that's exactly what I want to do; but I enjoy it so far." Allie responded.

"What does your boyfriend do?" Alex was getting a little braver.

"I actually just got out of a pretty long relationship. I had dated the same guy for three years. He is another reason why I needed something new this summer." Allie explained.

"I know what you mean. I just broke up with my girlfriend yesterday actually." Alex remarked.

"Let me guess, she's your ex-girlfriend." Allie pointed at the girl she recognized earlier.

"Marcy. Yeah, that's her. We have just been around each other for the past few summers so it was more like we dated because there were no other options. However, this summer I have seen some options so there is no need for me to be wasting time with her. You ready to jump in now?" Alex stood up and winked at Allie before hollering "cannon ball" and jumping in.

"Marcy." Allie said to herself. "That was the girl Skyler had mentioned being with Veronica." She remembered. "Obviously she's not over Alex." Allie was getting tired of the conversation in her head, so she stripped down to her bathing suit and jumped in mimicking Alex's cannon ball. The water was perfect, the company was great, and this was just what she needed.

Allie swam toward Skyler and climbed onto the large raft she was sharing with Braxton. Braxton rolled off the side to let the girls chat for a while.

"Alex, race you to the buoy." Braxton shouted as he and Alex swam as hard as they could trying not to be last.

"He's cute, isn't he?" Skyler asked Allie.

"Um, yeah, it's more than that though. I feel like he is someone I can just share anything with. I don't think I have ever felt that comfortable around someone that I didn't know." Allie sighed and smiled as she lay on her back starring up to the sky.

"Do you want me to tell you what I know?" Skyler asked Allie.

"About what?" Allie turned to look at Skyler.

"Alex. I am going to tell you anyway. He broke up with Marcy the day he saw you. He told Braxton that he thought you were pretty and that he was a sucker for long brown hair and hazel eyes. He is a little unsure about how you would feel about his age. I just want to put in a good word for him. He is a great guy." Allie smiled at all that Skyler was telling her.

Since they were sharing, Allie thought this would be a good idea to bring up the employee that was asking about her.

"Do you know anything about Billy Douglas. He manages the second floor buffet at the restaurant?" Allie decided just to come out and ask.

"I've heard Alex mention him. He said he was cool. I think they bowl together too." Skyler did seem to know everything about everything and everyone.

"But you've never seen him?" Allie questioned.

"No, I haven't why? Is he someone you are interested in?" It was obvious Skyler was hoping Allie was not interested.

"Actually he was asking me about you. He said he has had a crush on you since last summer. He wanted me to find out if you were seeing anyone and to let you know he was interested. He seems nice and pretty cute." Allie thought that a relationship with Billy might be better for Skyler than having a fling with Braxton.

"Guess I might have to check this guy out." Skyler raised her eyebrows and offered a crooked grin.

"ONE, TWO, THREE!" Alex and Braxton screamed as they dumped over the raft that Allie and Skyler were floating on.

Once Allie composed herself, she grabbed Alex and pushed him under. It was payback time. Allie was screaming and laughing for the first time in a long time.

Alex knew how to have a good time and perhaps by hanging around him this summer Allie would learn to do the same.

Allie glanced over to see if Skyler was having as much fun as she was. Allie saw a look on Skyler's face that she had not seen since they met. She was staring up toward the rocks at the figure of a guy and two girls. Allie strained her eyes to see if she could make out who these people were. She saw the guy was blond and it looked like he had a few visible tattoos. "That has to be Bobby." Allie thought to herself, but who were the girls. Moreover, if Skyler did not care about him, why was her face ashen and why was hurt showing in her eyes. There had to be more to the story.

"Are you okay?" Allie asked Skyler.

"I'm great. I am having a blast with you guys. I just do not understand how that jerk and those bimbos could come out here. That is Bobby, Katy, and Sarah. Katy is the girl that he cheated on me with. Whatever, I'm not even going to look over there." It was obvious that Skyler was annoyed and hurt, but it does take time for a heart to heal after it has been broken. Allie knew this and did not press the subject.

"Pizza at my place anyone?" Braxton offered only to Allie, Skyler, and Alex.

"Sounds good, we're in." Skyler replied for the group.

They swam back toward the bank, climbed out, and grabbed their things without any acknowledgement of Bobby and the girls. They took golf carts back to Braxton's cabin.

They were joking around, eating pizza, listening to music, and enjoying having the cabin to themselves for a little while. After one slice of store bought pizza and an hour of flirtation, Allie would have to call it a night.

"Goodnight guys, I have an early morning at the coffee shop, so I'll see you later. I had a great time." They said their goodbyes and suggested that they would do it again soon.

CHAPTER FIVE

It was a ridiculously hot morning as Allie headed off to work at the coffee shop. She was about to walk in the door when she heard a voice behind her.

"There you are." Allie turned around to see the same brown-eyed guy from the other night still wearing a cowboy hat and one of those sideways southern Virginia grins. Billy was coming to check up on any news that Allie was able to find out.

"She's definitely single. Her 'relationship' with Braxton is nothing serious, no titles just innocent flirting. Skyler is just trying to have fun, I brought your name up and she says she has heard Alex talk about you. I guess you guys bowl together or something. Anyway she plans on stopping by the restaurant soon to check you out and

Summer at The Point

introduce herself." Allie hoped he was happy with what she had to say.

"Great. I owe you one. Guess I need to look my best at work each night and try to impress her." His excitement showed all over his face.

"Well good luck. I am sure I will see you around. I've got to clock in." Allie headed inside for her first day as a barista.

Allie noticed a crowd was already starting to gather at the door before the coffee shop even opened. She was a little nervous but planned on smiling big and working hard to get the much needed tips she desired. Even though Allie had never worked at a coffee shop, Mr. Davis assured her that she would be fine as long as she had a love for coffee, strong customer skills, and the ability to multi-task.

"You must be Allie." Allie turned to see a lady who was older than the rest of the staff but had this essence about her that said she could definitely keep up. She had olive skin, long brown hair, and one heck of a bounce in her step for it to be so early in the morning.

"Hi! Yes I'm Allie." Something about this woman made Allie feel comforted. She was a motherly figure and Allie knew instantly that she could trust her.

"I'm Evelyn, but every one calls me Eve." Eve introduced herself to Allie. "I've been here for years, so if you have any questions about anything or anyone, feel free to ask."

"Okay, it's nice to meet you." Allie replied.

"You don't seem like the rest of the young girls here. I heard you took two jobs when most of the staff doesn't even want to work their one." It seemed as if Eve had already done her homework on Allie, but Allie wondered how she had not heard anything from Skyler about Eve.

"I took this job because I am trying to pay for school and any extra cash helps. Plus I left behind a big mess back home and I just need to get my mind off some things." For some reason Allie felt like opening up to Eve. Other than Alex, Allie has not mentioned anything to anyone about what she was leaving behind back home.

Eve showed Allie how to set up for the morning rush and placed cheat sheets to help her learn the specialty coffees. "The crowd is usually gone by eleven-thirty. Would you like to take a walk and talk on our break? I think it would be good for us to get to know each other. You seem like you really have your head on straight. That is rare to find around here. You remind me of Skyler Richardson, I am sure you have met her. You both seem to have a lot of ambition." Eve was making a great effort to get to know Allie and it was apparent they would become fast friends.

"I would love to talk, and yes I have met Skyler. We have hung out a couple of times." Allie looked up to see the crowd outside was getting restless. "Guess its time to get to work, the crowd looks like they definitely need some expresso." Allie wrapped her apron around her waist.

"Okay girl, I'll get the door." Eve switched the sign to open and unlocked the door. She spoke to everyone that entered as if they were all her close friends. Apparently, she did know everyone. Allie watched how Eve would greet every customer with a smile and offer assistance immediately. This was obviously something she has been doing for a long time.

Customers seemed to flow in continuously for the next five hours and then at eleven-thirty, just like Eve had said, the coffee shop was empty and they could take a break.

"Man, it seemed there was more than usual today. We will be slow now until twelve or so. I'm going to go smoke, care to join me." Eve motioned Allie to take a cigarette.

"No thanks. I'll go with you, but I don't smoke." Allie joined Eve on a picnic bench to the left of the coffee shop. You could see The Point from there and Allie smiled remembering how much fun she had there last night.

"So what made you decide to work here this summer?

We usually end up with the same bunch of local roughneck kids trying to get a free vacation and party with upper class socialites. Now, don't get me wrong, there are some good kids here too, real hard workers, and most of them are pretty attractive and entertaining. It can get to be like a little soap opera around here sometimes." She paused and looked to Allie eager to hear what she had to say.

"Well, I am going on my third year of college and I am running low on financial aid, so I needed to make some serious cash to pay rent. I saw an advertisement for this place online and I had heard the money was good. More importantly, it was away from college and home." Allie sighed and wondered if coming here really was the right thing. She knew that running away would not solve anything, but she hoped it would give her time to think.

"Why do you want to be away from home so bad? You could have made money at home, couldn't you?" Eve had a way of getting the answers she wanted.

"Yeah, I could have worked back home, but the truth is I wanted, or actually I needed, to get away from my ex-boyfriend. We had been together for around three years and things had gotten bad. When we broke up I needed a new start, something unfamiliar and exciting." Allie was finding that talking about this was becoming easier and it was helping her to figure things out. "Yep, a change of scenery, you know?"

"I understand completely. And I have to say, my nephew is a pretty nice guy, hard worker, and not unfortunate looking. When you're ready, I know he is interested. "Eve winked as she mentioned this to Allie.

"Do I know your nephew?" Allie was starting to think everyone around here was related.

"Alex." That was all Eve had to say to put a smile on Allie's face.

"He does seem to be a nice guy. Pretty popular with some of the girls around here too, it seems." Allie was still smiling. She was beginning to see a resemblance in Eve and Alex. It seems that he inherited her olive skin and brown hair, but his blue eyes were definitely unlike any she had seen before.

"He's single, just to put that out there. Anyway, guess we need to get back inside. Almost time for you to call it a day isn't it?" Eve headed back towards the door.

"Yes, I am done at noon." She looked at her watch.

"It's just about that time now. You can go clock out if you want. I can easily cover it from here." Eve stated.

 "It was good talking to you. Today was fun." Allie replied.

"When do you work again?" Eve asked.

"Not sure. I think I will be back in two days. I need to

check the new schedule." Allie said.

"Well I'll see you then. Remember what I said about Alex." Eve waived bye as Allie walked away from the coffee shop.

"Okay." Allie laughed and headed back toward her room to take a nap. The walk back gave Allie a chance to do some thinking. Could it be possible she was interested in a guy who was so much younger than her. What could they really have in common? She also wondered what Skyler was up to? She thought about going to find her when she got up from her nap, or perhaps she would go find Alex. After all, most of her new friends thought she should give him a chance. Maybe she will.

CHAPTER SIX

"So young lady, have you made any beneficial connections so far? You know that Reginald Billingsworth's son Arthur is visiting. He made the Dean's list his first year at Duke University. He plans to be a doctor, Skyler, and I'm sure he will be a wonderful one."

Skyler's father was always pushing her to get to know the socialites and their families. He thinks that if she meets the right boy, it will help her stay focused on her future. Mr. Billingsworth was the CEO of a toy company in northern California. He was Skyler's dad's best friend in college and they both bought vacation condos at the resort as a way to stay in contact. Mr. Billingsworth hardly ever visit's anymore, but his wife and children spend their summers at Rock Springs.

"Daddy, I don't know Mr. Billingsworth that well and I'm sure Arthur is great, but I have already made friends with some of the staff and..." She could not even finish her sentence before her father cut her off.

"The staff, Skyler, please. You need to associate yourself with go-getters, headhunters, those who know how to make it to the top. Not those who scrape the bottom of the barrel their whole lives trying to just get by." Skyler's dad only saw two types of people, those who were successful, meaning the rich, and those who lived to serve the rich.

"Father, you want me to go off to college in the fall, and what better way to adjust to college life than to get to know real college students. My friend Allie just finished her second year. She is going to be a nurse, and you know Braxton Davis, well father, his family is rather well. He does not even have to work, but he does. My friends have real character, father, and that is something the members lack. Besides, I want to be a singer anyway so why does it matter who I hang out with." Skyler was trying to defend herself and her friends, but her father stood firm behind his beliefs. "I know if you would just listen to me sing, then you would understand my passion."

"If that girl was smart, she wouldn't become a nurse. She would become a doctor or lawyer. And that boy, Braxton, he has no ambition. He is just sponging off of his father." Mr. Richardson proclaimed as he paced the floor. "Oh Skyler, a singer you will never get anywhere with those silly childhood dreams you continue to hang on to. I can never get through to you. You are hard headed like your mother." Skyler's dad walked away saying. "You are judged, my dear, by the company you keep. Remember that."

"Well then, I chose to keep my friends and those who want to judge me can do so. I would rather be happy and stay true to myself instead of trying to please others all the time." Skyler was annoyed and needed to talk to someone, so she grabbed an overnight bag and headed away from the condo. "My dreams are not silly, I have real talent and you would know that if you came to any of the karaoke contests in the past." Skyler said out loud to herself.

Skyler decided to walk toward the employee cabin to see what Allie was up to. She just needed to get out of the condo for a while.

******

"I absolutely love that outfit." Allie complimented her roommate as she awoke from her nap.

"Thanks, I designed it myself." D.J. replied as she applied her make-up. The frayed tan skirt and off the shoulder hot pink top complimented her dark complexion quite well. "I was thinking about going to the golf course to check out the caddies and maybe hit some balls at the driving range. Do you want to come along?" DJ asked as she pulled her hair back in a tight ponytail as always.

Allie thought this might be a good opportunity for her to get to know DJ and maybe meet some other employees. "Sure, just let me change."

The girls headed off to the golf course. As soon as they came around the corner of the cabin, there was Skyler. She was carrying a duffel bag and looked as if she were upset.

"Hey girl. Where are you headed?" Skyler asked Allie.

"We are headed out to the golf course to check out some guys. Would you care to join us?" Allie introduced her two friends. "This is D.J. by the way. She's my roommate this summer." Allie hoped Skyler would come along because she looked a little down. "Are you okay?"

"Oh me, I'm fine." Skyler assured Allie. "Good to meet you. I am Skyler. Sure, I will go with you guys. I need to do something away from my house and the parents. It's been a rough morning." Skyler was hurt and obviously needed to talk.

"Do you want to talk about what's going on with your parents?" Allie inquired.

"Not yet. Let's go look at boys and forget about our problems for a little while. Come on!" Skyler let out a yelp as she threw her bag over her shoulder and took off in a sprint down the hill.

47

The girls ran the whole mile to the golf course. They felt like kids as they giggled and sprinted across the resort.

"It's not easy to run that course in a skirt and flip-flops. But it was fun." D.J. said as she put her hands on her knees attempting to catch her breath.

"Yeah, I haven't sprinted like that since high school." Allie panted.

All Skyler could do was laugh, "I have never run like that, period!"

"Look girls. That is one good looking fella' standing by the golf carts. I claim that one, see you later." D.J. walked off heading toward a guy who seemed to be the male version of herself. He was tall, tanned, and blonde, wearing a pink polo and khaki shorts. The two of them looked like two models straight out of a catalogue .

"Well that didn't take long. Looks like it just the two of us again. Any idea who that guy was?" Allie asked as they walked away from D.J. and her new friend.

"Mike Carmichael. Our families are long time friends. I am surprised he is talking to your roommate. He is usually pretty stuck up. He tends to hang around Veronica's crowd. Anyway, now I can tell you a little more about what's bugging me." The two began to walk around the golf course. "It's my dad. He doesn't like me hanging out with the staff and Braxton. He is trying to set me up with one of the member's sons. He is really starting to bug me." Skyler was plotting something. She wanted to get back at her dad and make him realize that she was going to do whatever made her happy and she was not interested in any plans he had made for her.

"I figured it was something like that bothering you. Anything you need me to do?" Allie offered her help, hoping Skyler would realize that she would be there for her no matter what.

"I want my dad to realize how much I love singing. He has always said that it was a waste of time and not a real skill. Well, they are having the annual karaoke contest this Friday night. It is going to be at the restaurant and I am planning on competing again this year. My dad has never been, but this time he will be there meeting with the Carmichaels and Mr. Billingsworth. Braxton and I will perform a duet, so he will be there. I want you and Alex there too. I want my dad to see me doing something I am passionate about and also see that I have real friends who support me." Skyler wanted to show off and let everyone know how determined she was to pave her own way.

"Okay. I didn't know you sang. That is wonderful! I will back you one hundred percent. I'm working that night, so I'll definitely be there. Let's go get your name on the list." Allie was excited that

Skyler was going to sing in the contest. She also

Summer at The Point

thought about using that night to introduce her to Billy too.

Allie and Skyler walked back to the golf carts. They looked for D.J. to let her know where they were headed, but she was nowhere around.

"D.J. must have gone off with Mike. I just hope Veronica doesn't pop up and ruin it for her." Skyler remarked.

Since Skyler had left her golf cart back at the condo, they swiped a rental. Then, they headed to the registration desk to put Skyler's name on the karaoke list. Skyler drove the cart toward the main entrance of the resort toward the registration office. "I look forward to the karaoke contest every year. I'm pretty excited."

The hopped off the golf cart and ran into the office. No one was at the desk, so Skyler reached behind the counter to grab the sign-up book. She read over the list of names to see who else had signed up. The first name on the list was Veronica, of course. She also recognized most .

"Anyone I know singing?" Allie asked.

"Veronica is on here along with some of the other regulars. That guy Billy that you want me to meet is on here too. He is fifth on the list, but he doesn't have a song title listed yet. Guess I will get to see him sooner than I thought. What should I sing?" Skyler was thinking out loud trying to think of what song she did best. "I need a song that makes a statement, I've got it." Skyler jotted down her name with the song title and put the book back in its spot. "I'm not going to stay at the condo tonight. Do you want to stay with me at Braxton's?"

"I can. I just need to pack a bag. I work lunch and early dinner tomorrow." Allie remarked as they headed back outside.

"Okay let's go get your things and then we'll go find Braxton." Skyler jumped back on the golf cart and motioned for Allie to do the same.

"Will we see Alex tonight?" Allie surprised herself when she let that question out.

"Sure will." Skyler replied as she grinned at Allie.

CHAPTER SEVEN

Billy starred in the mirror really who he was and how he could impress Skyler. He was wearing his favorite blue polo and a pair of white washed jeans. "What do they have that I don't?" he asked his reflection. Bobby was a rebel and the way he treated Skyler showed a lack of character. Skyler's dad did not even know about the relationship she had with Bobby. Billy knew he did not want to be that guy. Then there was Braxton. He was young and unconventional, but not nearly man enough for Skyler.

"I would be good for her." Billy said as he continued to talk to the mirror and build his confidence. The karaoke contest was coming up on Friday and Billy knew that would be his chance to catch Skyler's eye. He had no idea yet what he was going to sing, but he knew he had to make his mind up soon. He thought that perhaps a country love hit, older rock, or pop song. Billy paced around his room as he contemplated his song choice.

"I've got it!" Billy thought out loud. He remembered a country song where a guy is singing about his crush. The song describes the girl as having her mother's good looks, her dad's money, and a killer personality, which sounds exactly like Skyler. He thought the song would be fun and not too serious that it would scare Skyler off. "But then again, I need something to show off my vocals and personality, " he thought. Billy put on his college fraternity ring and cowboy hat then headed out the door still contemplating his song title. He knew he would make up his mind by the time he got to the Reservation Office. His name was already on the list, he just needed the song title.

Billy had just graduated from the Virginia Tech where he received a degree in Hospitality and Tourism Management. His long-term goal is to be a manager of a private resort or hotel one day, but right now, he was concentrating on learning the ropes, and networking with members at the resort. Billy had some job offers coming out of school, but he wanted to have one more summer at Rock Springs. This summer, he is acting as second floor kitchen manager, and hopes to continue to climb the ladder to a higher position. The second floor was the buffet at night and snack shack during the day. Alex and Braxton work in the first floor kitchen where the actual restaurant and bar are located. Even though Billy was not on the floor with menus and the bar, the buffet gave him a chance to be creative. More importantly, it was a chance to act as a manager, adding more experience to his resume.

Billy decided to take the long way up to the office so he could have more time alone with his thoughts, and mentally prepare for Friday night. He made his way along the broken trails, and imagined the outcome of Friday night's contest.

Billy had stopped to tie his shoe when he heard footsteps coming up behind him.

"Billy, is that you?" Billy looked up and noticed a familiar face approaching him. "Remember me, Marcy. I used to date Alex. I met you last summer when you and Alex were on the bowling league." Billy never cared too much for Marcy, and he was surprised she was attempting to carry on a conversation with him.

"I remember you. I'm on my way somewhere, Excuse me." Billy attempted to walk by Marcy. He knew her family and he knew she was trouble. However, most importantly, he knew that Marcy did not get along with Skyler.

"I'll see you Friday night though, right? You are singing in the contest." Marcy jumped in front of Billy to hold him up once again.

"Yes. I'm sorry Marcy. I need to get going." This time he did not give her a chance to cut him off. He continued on his way without any further acknowledgement of

Summer at The Point

Marcy.

It took about fifteen minutes for Billy to get to the Reservation Office. When he walked in, he saw Alex behind the counter filling in while the regular receptionist was on her lunch break.

"You are everywhere man." Billy said to Alex. He was glad that he was working instead of the usual desk clerk. Billy was still a little embarrassed about his singing and he knew Alex was less likely to make fun of what he was getting into.

"Yeah, just trying to fill in when I can. Plus, it keeps Marcy off my tail. How is it going so far this summer dude? You graduated didn't you." Alex thought a lot of Billy and admired the fact that he was a college graduate and a hard worker.

"Summer is going pretty good. I graduated this May and it is nice to be finished. It is a little unnerving in the real world, but it is going to get better I'm sure. So, you and Marcy are over?" Billy was glad, but he wondered what had happed between the two of them. From what Billy had heard, Alex and Marcy have always been together.

"Yeah, I broke things off with her. I'm actually talking to one of the girls working here this summer." Alex confessed.

"Good for you, man." Billy replied.

Summer at The Point

"We hung out last night and a few times before. She's cool. She's in college though. I don't really know how she feels about my age." Alex had a feeling Allie was concerned about his age. He knew he needed to make her see past that, and he hoped Billy would offer some encouragement.

"A new girl, huh? Is it someone I would know?" Billy inquired.

"Allie. She is a waitress on first floor. She's been hanging around with Skyler, Braxton, and me." Alex thought about Allie for a minute and smiled. "This one is special, man."

"I know Allie. She has been helping me out with something. Very nice. You should go for it. Who cares about age? What is the difference anyway, two years?" Billy did not know if the two of them would work out, but he always supported his friends.

"Three years actually." Alex looked down. "I don't know, man. I want to hang out with someone different and fun. I think we would have a good time together. Maybe, she'll come around. Well, like I said, I don't know." Alex was rambling, but Billy understood, after all he was the same way when rationalizing the idea of Skyler and himself.

"I have to say, I'm in a similar predicament." Billy felt like if he told Alex about his crush on Skyler then at least he would have someone else supporting him. It did worry him however, that Alex was Braxton's friend and telling him could be a negative thing. "I have been trying to catch Skyler Richardson's eye since last summer. I think she is amazing, dude. In fact, she is the only reason that I am singing in the karaoke contest." Billy decided he did not care if Alex told Braxton. He just needed to let his feelings out. "That's how I know Allie. She has been helping me find out more about Skyler."

"Oh, okay. Well, I have to say I would rather her be with you than Braxton. Skyler and I go way back and she has always been with guys who were bad for her. I think you should go for her and let her know how you feel. Braxton is my boy, but he is a flirt and he is never serious about anything, especially girls. He might surprise me, but I doubt it." Alex was welcoming to this idea and thought it would be cool to hang out with Billy and Skyler as a couple.

Billy still had not decided on a song title and he was getting frustrated. "I need help picking a song for the contest." Billy blurted out as he looked up and saw the desk clerk returning from her break.

Quickly Alex jotted down a song title on a piece of paper. "What about this one? Do you know it?"

"Perfect." Billy did not know why he had not thought of that one sooner.

Alex recorded the song title in the book and returned it before heading out the door with Billy. "Well man, it's done. I will catch you later. I am going to go catch a nap at Braxton's place. Good luck with everything, I got your back man." Alex broke out into a jog as he headed toward Braxton's dad's cabin.

Billy headed back down the same long path back to his room. He wanted to change and head to the pool for a little while before work.

"Everything will work out. Friday is going to be a great night." He thought to himself and grinned as he thought of singing to Skyler.

CHAPTER EIGHT

"Hey girl! What brings you out here?" Allie was setting tables for the dinner rush when she looked up and saw Skyler. She seemed nervous and looked like she needed to talk. "What's wrong, Skyler?" Allie asked.

"Do you have a second?" Skyler asked Allie while motioning toward the waitress station.

"Sure." Allie put down the silverware and walked toward Skyler. Dinner did not start for another hour so there was no rush to set the tables. "Is everything alright?"

"Yeah, everything is fine. I am just a little worried about

something, and I wanted to run it by you."

"Yeah, okay sure." Allie consented.

"Well, Braxton is off tonight and has the cabin to himself. He, um, wants to fix me dinner and watch movies. You know, hang out, just the two of us." Skyler appeared to be having a mini anxiety attack. "I like him, you see, but I don't want to be with him. I mean he is cooking for me and everything. It just doesn't seem like he is being the same laidback, carefree guy from before." Skyler looked around and noticed Braxton's dad glaring at the two of them as if timing how long Allie was sitting. "I'm sorry girl. It's a bad time I know. Should I go?"

Allie ignored Mr. Davis. "If you have mixed feelings, you need to tell him. I would meet him in an attempt to spare his feelings, but make it very clear that you do not want to put labels on your relationship. Maybe you should head up to second floor and see Billy." Allie smiled. "I'm just kidding. Go with your gut, and if you need me, come back. I'll be off by nine tonight. I can swing by and check on you if you want?"

"Please come by and make sure everything is cool. I am going to go and just explain what I feel. Thanks. I have to head up to third floor first and pick up a menu from the Catering Director. My mom is hosting a get-together with some of the members Saturday night and she wants to make sure the menu is up to par. I'll see you later. Thanks again." Skyler stood up, took a deep breath and headed toward the elevator. Before getting on, she looked back at Allie. It looked as if Braxton's dad was explaining something to her. Skyler hoped she did not get her in trouble.

Skyler got on the elevator and headed up to the third level. This was probably Skyler's favorite floor in the four level building. The third floor was not only where the caterer's office was, but also where all of the resort mixer's take place. There was a dance floor and sound system to the right, which extended out into a sunroom. The view from the sunroom overlooked the entire resort. You could see the water as well as the beautiful green of the golf course. To the left of the elevator were two pool tables and an air hockey table. At the back center, right by the hall entrance for the office, there was a stage where Skyler won runner-up last summer in the Miss Rock Springs pageant. She remembered the pageant and losing to Veronica, but she shrugged it off and headed to the office. She knew that this year's pageant would be different and the summer would end with her being Miss Rock Springs.

The door was locked with a note saying that Mrs. Applegate was gone for the day due to illness. Skyler had plans, of course, so she was in a hurry and did not feel like tracking anyone down to get the menus out of the office. She jiggled the handle a little just to see if she could get in. It was locked but she noticed the lock was similar to the one on her bedroom door at the condo. Skyler knew that all she needed was a stiff

Summer at The Point

piece of paper, and a dime and she could get the door open. She walked back toward the stage and noticed a pile of supplies on the small table. She figured they must have been left by the Activities Director. "Perfect." Skyler remarked as she picked up exactly what she needed.

Once in the office, Skyler flicked on the light, and began to look for the menu. It was right on top, and had her mother's name listed in the corner. She cut the light off and headed back out. As she closed the door, she noticed that the office at the back of the hall had a light on. She could hear two male voices coming from behind the door.

"Thanks for the offer Mr. Parks. I think that will work out great. I appreciate it." One of the voices stated as he prepared to leave the office.

"Oh, no." Skyler recognized that voice, so headed immediately toward the elevator. It was Bobby. He was talking with the Membership Director, Mr. Parks. He was probably negotiating a way to stay on the resort without paying membership.

She got on the elevator alone, nervous at the thought of meeting Braxton, and afraid of what tonight could mean for the two of them. As the elevator closed, a tattooed arm reaches in to reopen the doors just in time. There he was, Bobby Shea.

"Hi you." He said as he looked at Skyler.

At first, she does not speak, and there was an awkward silence. Then a jolt catches them both off guard. The elevator stopped. Frantically Skyler hits the buttons trying to open the doors. This was a disaster in more ways than one. Not only was she stuck on an elevator with her ex, but she was going to be late meeting Braxton.

"This sucks." Skyler said annoyed.

"Ah, she speaks." Bobby grinned.

"Trust me, you don't want to hear me speak, jerk." Skyler could feel the rage building inside of her as she thought about all the pain Bobby had caused her. Skyler continued to fiddle with the buttons. "Uh, why isn't there an emergency button or phone in this stupid thing?"

"Chill out girl. It is all good. You do know that everything happens for a reason. Fate put us on this elevator together." Bobby continued to grin at Skyler. "Someone will realize it's stuck and be here soon to fix it."

"No one uses this thing after five, bonehead. And, since there are two of them, it's a slim chance anyone will notice." Skyler sat on the floor and tucked her head between her knees.

"Mr. Parks is still upstairs. He will probably figure it out. But until then, maybe we could catch up." Bobby sat next to Skyler and put his arm around her. "Come on beautiful, smile for me."

Skyler pushed him away and slid over. "I don't want to talk to you Bobby. Let's just sit here and think of a way to get out."

"How about I talk then, and you just listen." Bobby had a lot he needed to get off his chest. He has been wrapped with guilt ever since he cheated on Skyler and now he would finally have a chance to tell her. "I'm sorry. I do not think I ever got a chance to tell you that. But what did you expect Skyler, you never even told your parents about us. I felt like I was never good enough for you. Plus, you were gone for six months. I had no clue what you were doing, or who you were meeting. I was unhappy and fed up." Bobby looked hurt as he confessed his side of the story to Skyler.

She did not want to hear this, but she did not stop him from sharing. It was nice to see a sentimental side of Bobby for a change. It showed that maybe he did really care, or then again, he could just be trying to gain her sympathy and weasel his way back into her life.

"Are you really sorry, Bobby? I mean you seem to be happy with your new crowd of friends. I saw you with them at The Point." Skyler did want some answers but she did not want to be so aggressive that he would pull away.

"I am sorry, and yes, I am happy. Don't get me wrong. I

miss you like crazy. It is just that it has been over six months since I um, well you know. I have gotten close with Katy, Sarah, and the rest of their friends. Even Mr. Parks has been cool, letting me crash at his place no charge, as long as I help a couple days a week in maintenance. But anyway, I'm sorry about the way you found out about everything with Katy." Bobby confessed.

"Yeah, it was pretty low of Katy to send me a video email of the two of you while I was with mother in France. Figures Katy would do something like that. Well anyway, it was New Year's Eve right. At least you waited that long before you cheated." Skyler responded as she rolled her eyes. "And I dumped you in a similar manner, remember? I sent you a video email with me dumping you with one of the most beautiful cities in the world in the background. Whatever, its over and done. I don't even want to think about it anymore." Skyler stood up and walked to the opposite side of the elevator.

"Okay, of course, I remember you breaking up with me. Actually, at the time, I didn't know that Katy had sent that video to you. I didn't find that out until recently." Bobby explained. "Let's move past it, can't we. I'm sorry you got hurt. I thought that the break up was the right thing. It made sense, and I didn't think it would be to hard on either of us since we were so far apart. But, when I saw you at The Point the other night and seeing you now, well, I still feel something for you. Let's forget the past and at least rebuild our friendship." Bobby walked over toward Skyler as she stood with her back against the wall. He hugged her and surprisingly she let him. Having Bobby close to her still felt good, and she couldn't deny that.

******

Meanwhile, back at Mr. Davis's cabin, Braxton was preparing for his special night with Skyler. There were rose petals scattered on the floor, and the room smelled as if he had captured the scent of a warm spring day and released it into the cabin. There were chocolate dipped strawberries spread out on a platter in front of the sofa. He had placed a picnic basket on a blanket, filled with other fruits and finger foods. Braxton had also managed to get his hands on a bottle of wine that his dad had been hiding in the cabinet behind the oatmeal.

"Deep breath." Braxton said out loud, as he looked in the mirror at himself. He had never been nervous about hanging out with a girl, but he had also never been this crazy over one either. They were just supposed to be having fun this summer, no rules, no relationships. What changed? He hoped she wanted this; he hoped she was ready. Who knew years of innocent flirting would lead to this?

Six-thirty came and went. Braxton started to ponder the idea that maybe she wasn't coming. Maybe she was standing him up. No, that couldn't be right. "She wouldn't leave me hanging." He thought out loud. He sat on the couch and started watching television to take his mind off of the clock.

After a little TV, a frustrated Braxton looked up to see that it was now seven-thirty and still no sign of Skyler. He began to wonder if maybe he should go look for her. "She could have gotten the time mixed up. Maybe she thought eight o'clock." Braxton thought to himself.

Braxton was getting hungry, so he started snacking on the food he had set aside for Skyler and himself to enjoy together. He pushed play on the movie while popping open the bottle of wine. "Cheers," Braxton held his glass up towards the television and took a sip. He was three glasses in before he realized that she definitely was not coming. He then grabbed a ball cap and headed out the door. "The heck with this, I'm out of here," he remarked.

"Whoa, where are you headed? Where's Skyler?" Allie said as Braxton bumped into her when storming out of the door. It was now nine-fifteen and Allie was dropping by like Skyler asked.

"She never showed and you know what? I don't even care." Braxton walked away from Allie.

His stench took Allie's breath away as she caught a whiff of his cologne. "Wait! Something must be wrong. I saw her earlier and she was on her way to meet you." Allie was starting to get worried.

Summer at The Point

"When did you see her? Where?" Braxton was no longer angry, instead he became concerned.

"Around four. She was up at the restaurant. She said that she needed to go by the caterer's and then she would be going to meet you."

"Should we go back to the restaurant and start looking for her? I'm worried now." Braxton grabbed a flash light and walked over toward his golf cart. "Come on, this will be faster."

They jumped on the golf cart and started toward the restaurant. Braxton was taking those hairpin turns a little too quickly for Allie, but she held on and dealt with it. "It's going to be okay Braxton. We are going to find her. She may have gotten tied up with her parents or something."

After parking, they ran towards the back door employee entrance so they wouldn't draw any attention to themselves.

"In a hurry, are we?" Katy was sitting on a picnic table across from the entrance.

"What are you doing back here? Shouldn't you be off somewhere with Bobby." Braxton said in a hateful way.

"Oh please, you just wish you still had me." Katy stood up and walked toward him. "Anyway, no one has been able to find Bobby since earlier this afternoon. He met with Mr. Parks around four or so and we haven't seen

68

him since."

Allie was really confused now. Apparently, everyone here dates in circles. It really was the 'mini soap opera' Eve had described.

"Wait! Bobby has been missing since four. Hah, so has Skyler. Wonderful, now I'm ticked off again. I swear, if he has done something to her, I'll kick his butt." Braxton punched the side of the building.

"Calm down you two. Braxton, don't do that crap, you'll break your hand." Allie punched his arm to make her point. "We don't know anything for sure. Let's go up to third floor and start there." Allie tried to reason with Katy and Braxton, but there was no point. Both of them were extremely irritated.

They walked in the building, headed over to the elevators, and pushed the button. Ten minutes passed before the elevator finally arrived. "Man, that thing is slow. Dad needs to do something about that." Braxton remarked.

When they got off on the third floor, they split up. No one was up there, and all lights were off. They could have taken the stairs down to second, but they headed toward the elevator instead. It was the same elevator that they took before, and it once again took forever to arrive. "I want to check something out guys hold on. This is the only elevator I have seen working today. Take it down to second and wait on me." Allie suggested.

Katy and Braxton got on the elevator and headed to the second floor. Twenty minutes later Allie finally made it down to the floor. "Did the other elevator open at all?" Allie questioned.

"Naw. The one you got off of let some folks off, but the other never did." Braxton said. "Dude, are you trying to say that elevator is stuck."

"Yep. I bet Skyler is on it too." Allie stated. "We need to go get maintenance."

"Leroy is on duty tonight, I saw him napping in his golf cart down behind the building. I'll go get him. Do you think Bobby might be in there too?" Katy asked as she took off down the stairs to find Leroy before Allie could reply.

Ten minutes passed and Katy returned with a man who appeared to be in his late thirties. He had on a pair of ratty, paint-stained jeans that sat below his waist just enough for his protruding belly to hang over. Allie also noticed that he smelled strong of cigarette smoke. His accent was thick, southern, and slow as he asked Katy a few yes or no questions.

"He's been here for nearly ten years. And yes, he has always looked like that." Braxton whispered only to Allie knowing what she was thinking. "Hey man, the elevator is jammed. Can you fix it?"

"Uh, yeah. Give me about half an hour and I'll have it done. Anyone on it?" Leroy asked Braxton.

"We think Skyler might be on it, but we don't know for sure." Braxton replied.

Allie and Braxton sat on the staircase watching Leroy work. They were trying to stay out of his way, and avoid the rest of the madness going on in the restaurant as well. Katy didn't care though, she was pacing around behind Leroy rushing him to finish.

Finally, Leroy put down his tools. "Done." He stood up and hit both the up and down button.

As the elevator dinged and the doors opened, everyone gathered around to look it.

"Oh my goodness!! Katy shrieked. "You jerk!"

"You have to be kidding me." Braxton chimed in.

Allie was caught off guard as well. When she looked in, she saw Bobby seated up against the back wall and Skyler was lying in his lap. Both of them were asleep until they heard the angry squeals from their dates.

Skyler got up first, looked at Braxton, and began to explain herself. "I hope you don't think... we have been in there for hours. No! Braxton, I just needed to lie down. You know I hate Bobby now." Skyler tried to hug Braxton.

"I can't talk to you right now." Braxton left in a rush. He ran out the door, grabbed the golf cart and headed back to the cabin.

Katy wasn't as upset once Bobby started to explain his side of the story. He reminded her of how much he cared for her, and how he must have fallen asleep before Skyler lay in his lap. "It's okay sweetie, I love you. I know how she is." Katy smiled as she spoke to Bobby. "Let's get out of here." They headed out as well. Katy was quick to get Bobby away from Skyler.

"Allie, I didn't mean for this to happen. I wasn't going to stand up Braxton. I feel terrible." Skyler confessed.

"He'll get over it. Just let him cool off and you can explain it to him later. Plus, you didn't want a relationship with him anyway, right?" Allie was trying to be helpful.

"You're right, but I didn't want to hurt him either. By the way, nothing happened. We talked a little about the past, but that was it." Skyler just couldn't get her head straight. "I need to get out of here. Want to go down to The Point for a little while?"

"I would, but I have to work at the Coffee Shop in the morning. Plus, karaoke is tomorrow night, so I need some rest. You can stay with me and DJ tonight if you need to." Allie didn't want to leave her friend like this, but she was pretty tired and she had a long day ahead of her tomorrow.

"It's okay. I should go back to my parent's place anyway. I'll come to the Coffee Shop tomorrow, if that's okay." Skyler and Allie started walking to the exit.

"Yeah, that's fine. I get off at noon, and I don't have to be at the restaurant until six." Allie was going to use that time to find Alex, but if Skyler needed her, she would be there.

"Well, my golf cart is in the front. Let me give you a ride back to your room." Skyler offered.

"That would be great. Thanks girl." Allie was glad she wouldn't have to do anymore walking across the resort tonight.

Skyler pulled up to the cabin. As Allie was attempting to get off, she noticed Billy off in the distance. She quickly looked away acting as if she didn't see him. Tonight just wasn't the night to introduce him to Skyler. Allie said goodbye to Skyler, and made a hard left toward the side entrance of the living quarters.

"Tomorrow is a new day. I'll worry with it then." She thought to herself hoping to feel less guilty about ignoring Billy.

Summer at The Point

CHAPTER NINE

She was sitting on one of the big rocks at The Point looking out over the lake, and remembering why she used to love this place so much. It was just after sunrise and some of the lifeguards were swimming laps by the dock. Skyler took a deep breath in, filling her lungs with air and head with memories. She could see the old playground in the distance. That was where she got her first kiss years ago. Of course, it was Braxton Davis. He was eleven and she was thirteen. Skyler let out a small laugh as she thought about how even at that young age he was already a smooth talker. Then as she rolled her eyes, she remembered his curly, out of control hair that she used to find so adorable.

Skyler could see Leroy backing the mower off the truck behind the playground. She knew that Allie and Eve would be coming down the hill shortly to get ready for the morning coffee rush. She wondered what Allie would say to her when she noticed that Skyler was wearing the same clothes from last night. Skyler laid back on the rock just starring up at the sky. She couldn't believe she had spent the entire night on that rock. There are just times when you want to be alone. Even your best friends or family can't always fill the void when you're confused and hurting. Skyler closed her eyes and continued to sort out her thoughts.

"Oh My!" Allie screamed as jogged towards The Point. "It is you. Have you been here all night?" Allie asked even though she knew the answer once she noticed Skyler was still in last night's clothes. "Leroy flagged down Eve as she was on her way to the coffee shop. He said that saw someone sleeping out on the rocks. He told us that we should come check it out. Are you alright, Skyler?"

Skyler was slow to sit up. "I'm fine. Must have dozed off again. Yeah, well, um, anyway I have been out here all night trying to get my thoughts together." Skyler twisted her torso in an attempt to pop her sore back. "I just couldn't go back to my parent's place after last night. Do you have a minute to sit and talk?" Skyler looked at Allie as if she really needed her to stay and listen.

"Sure. I can sit for a while, not much of a crowd this morning anyway. So tell me Skyler, what is going on up there?" Allie pushed her index finger against Skyler's forehead.

"I just hate that I hurt Braxton. I know that I was unsure about spending time with him last night, but I never would have stood him up on purpose. I hope he understands that I no longer have any interest in Bobby and that last night was just a big mix-up. Braxton has known me for so long and he has always been there for me. I hate to lose that." Allie offered a compassionate pat on the shoulder showing her concern. "Should I talk to him?" Skyler had obviously been crying at some point this morning. Allie could tell that from her swollen, blood-shot eyes.

"Talk to him Skyler. Let him know that you are sorry about the way everything turned out. Tell him how much you value his friendship. I honestly think he will be more rationale today. He should understand that it is not something that you planned. He overreacted Skyler, you didn't do anything wrong." Allie wondered how Bobby and Katy were getting along today.

"Maybe, I just feel like I let Braxton down and that kills me, you know? Even though I had no control over what happened, I feel like Braxton will never trust me like he used to. What the rest of the resort thinks, including my parents, does not even matter. All that matters is my friendship with Braxton." Skyler got up and attempted to pop her back a second time. She was extremely sore from spending the night on that rock and she knew she needed a nap in a real bed before the contest.

"I really don't think it's going to be a big deal. Why don't you stop by and see Braxton on your way back? Talk it out with him and figure out what you two really want from each other. This whole event might be a blessing in disguise." Allie gave Skyler an assuring hug. "It will be fine. You'll be fine."

"Thanks. I'll be up at the restaurant around six or so to get ready for the contest. I'll fill you in if I talk with Braxton. See you then." Skyler responded.

Skyler walked slowly toward the tennis courts to retrieve her golf cart. She left with her head still in the clouds. Last night still seemed like a bad dream.

******

The cabin looked empty. There were no golf carts in the driveway, and it looked as if all the doors were locked. Skyler almost turned back, but something told her she needed to go in and settle this. She parked her golf cart and walked around to the back door. She could see that someone was lying on the couch. Skyler was about to knock when the person on the couch started to get up. Now she noticed that there were actually two people on that couch. She backed up and stood to the side so that she could not be seen. Skyler could not believe that Braxton was already with someone else. When she saw who it was her stomach turned. Marcy, of all people got up from the couch and sat on the coffee table facing Braxton.

"Good morning." Marcy was gleaming and attempting to wake Braxton.

"Why are you here? Ah, man my head is killing me. Wait, just go home Marcy. I don't even want to hear why you're here." Braxton was angry and had obviously finished off his dad's wine, and the empty beer cans on the table proved he had also consumed a six-pack.

Skyler couldn't help but grin while listening to Braxton kick Marcy out. She was curious about why she was there, and especially why she was on the couch. But right now, she was enjoying the conversation.

"Braxton, what is wrong with you? You said you wanted to talk. You asked me to stay." Marcy was beginning to whine.

"I didn't ask you to stay, Marcy. You were here when I got here. I should have kicked you out then, but I was upset. I remember drinking and ranting about Skyler. I don't remember asking you to be here for me." Braxton was really starting to get angry. "I'll throw you out if I have to. Leave!"

"You know she doesn't care about you. She'll always love Bobby. You are just wasting your time." Marcy walked to grab her phone.

"You don't even know her. I could say the same about you, you know. Alex cannot stand you, and I cannot stand you. Get away from me." Braxton picked up the empty wine bottle and threw it at the door. Marcy shrilled when the glass shattered.

Skyler busted through the door once she saw Braxton was losing his temper. "Okay, I've seen enough! Look you little half-wit bimbo, get out! Braxton's right, you don't know any of us, and we surely don't want to know you!"

"Ha. Classic Skyler, in yesterdays clothes nonetheless. Funny how I was the one here last night when he got home. Where were you? Out with Bobby perhaps?" Marcy was getting a little too overconfident and cocky, which made Skyler pop her knuckles in preparation for a possible fight.

"Where I was doesn't concern you. And the only reason you were here is because you were trying to find Alex, but he keeps blowing you off. Maybe that should tell you something. Get a life Marcy!" Skyler snatched Marcy's phone out of her hands and threw it out the door. As Marcy walked out after it, Skyler slammed the door behind her. "Just keep walking."

Skyler started to pick the glass up off the floor. Thank goodness, Braxton's dad was already at work. "So guess we both have things to explain, huh?"

"I don't think I need to explain anything. You know that I would never be with Marcy. She was here when I got home and I was upset. I went to sleep and I thought

she had gone home." Braxton was apologetic even though he didn't feel like he owed her anything.

"Braxton, we really do need to talk. Actually, I need to talk. I was coming to meet you last night, I didn't plan on the elevator breaking down, and I definitely didn't plan on Bobby being there. I am going to be honest with you. Even though I was coming to hang out with you, I was having second thoughts." Skyler spoke out about what had been bothering her. "This summer was supposed to be fun with no strings attached just like it has always been with us. I was afraid you wanted a relationship with me and that isn't what we had planned. Braxton, you mean so much to me as a friend and I don't want to mess that up." Skyler felt a lot better talking about all that she had been holding in. She wanted to offer more of an explanation, but she was pretty sure Braxton understood.

"I didn't know what I wanted Skyler, and I still don't. I just thought that you deserved a romantic night. Honestly, I guess it was me trying to be someone I'm not. I know that you deserve so much more than I can offer you right now and I know that we have a great friendship. But I still can't help that I'm attracted to you." Braxton reached out to pull Skyler close to him.

He smelled of alcohol, stale cigarettes, and cologne making Skyler back away very quickly. "Let's just be friends right now, okay? I just need your friendship Braxton." She didn't know if this was really going to work, after all she has never been able to resist Braxton.

"Great, yeah, friends. Okay." Braxton was obviously disappointed. He walked away, "I'll see you tonight then."

"How about our duet? Are you still going to sing with me?" Skyler was afraid she had just pushed Braxton away.

"No, yeah, I'll still do it. I'll pick you up close to six. We can still ride together, right?" Braxton didn't know how the new 'friendship' was going to work out.

"That sounds great." Skyler hugged Braxton bye and turned for the door. "Just one more thing." Skyler kissed Braxton one last time to make sure she had made the right decision. Then she pulled away quickly and sprinted out to her golf cart. "Just friends," she reminded herself. "That's all we can ever be." Skyler thought as she assured herself that any romantic involvement with Braxton was now officially over.

"Women, go figure." Braxton stated as he plopped back down on the couch to catch a nap.

CHAPTER TEN

One by one, the contestants and customers began to file into the restaurant for the night's festivities. Tickets were sold to locals and the resort was expecting around one hundred non-members to be in the audience. Allie was still setting the tables and Leroy was finishing up with the stage and lights. All of the restrooms in the building were being used as dressing rooms for the performers. Every year contestants go all out on their make-up and wardrobe in order to impress the judges and claim victory. This year there was an extra incentive for winning the karaoke contest. The resort is offering one thousand dollars to the winner. For the members, the contest prize money was not what they are after. Bragging rights, however, that was what they are competing for.

Allie saw Veronica and her entourage heading into the bathroom by the elevator, and some of the caddies had formed a group, and were practicing their vocals next to the staircase. Allie began to set up the judges table that was located to the right of the stage next to her waitress station. Since a large crowd was expected, all of the wait staff were working, including Eve from the coffee shop.

"Lots of tips expected for tonight. Plus it should be a lot of fun." Eve said to Allie.

"Yeah, I'm nervous, but tonight should definitely be entertaining. I just hope the drama stays at a minimum. After all I..." Allie stopped short and her faced turned a ghostly shade of white.

"Allie! What's wrong?" Eve was shaking Allie, trying to regain her attention. "Do you know him?" Eve noticed that Allie was focused on a young man at the front door. He appeared to be in his early twenties. Ball cap, t-shirt, and tennis shoes gave him away to be one of the paying non-member customers. "Would you like me to go seat him?"

Allie didn't answer any of Eve's questions. She just sat the silverware down and began to walk towards the mysterious guy at the door. Once the young man noticed Allie walking towards him, he began to look down at the floor as if he was ashamed.

"Why are you here, Eric? How did you get on the resort?" Allie's stomach was knotted up and she just wanted a simple answer.

"I bought a ticket for the Karaoke contest. I needed to see you. We need to talk Allie. You don't return my calls, and you just left Greenville without even letting me try to fix things. I don't know why you broke up with me. I went by your house, and your sister told me I could find you here." Eric's oversized ego was apparently bruised.

"You shouldn't be here Eric. You know why I ended things. Please leave." Allie turned to walk away from Eric.

"Get back here!" He shouted as he grabbed her arm and pulled her back.

"Let go of me Eric! You're causing a scene." Allie tried to keep her voice low and wiggle out of Eric's grasp.

"I'll show you a scene. You're coming with me." Eric began to drag Allie towards the door.

"Hey buddy! I think she said back off!" Alex stood face to face with Eric as if he was challenging him to do something. "You need to leave dude."

"And who the hell are you?" Eric demanded.

"Security. Hers." Alex turned to wink at Allie.

84

"It's okay Alex. Eric was just leaving. Weren't you Eric?" Allie didn't want any kind of drama. She just wanted to pretend as if nothing had happened.

"Babe, I'm not leaving here without you. Tell bouncer boy to back off so we can talk." Eric reached his hand out to Allie.

"I'll be fine Alex." Allie shook her head to assure Alex. "Will you see if Eve needs any help? I'm going to step outside for a couple of minutes to speak with Eric, but I'll be back." Allie hugged Alex. "Come after me please if I'm not back in ten." Allie whispered in Alex's ear.

Allie and Eric walked through the double doors of the main entrance and Allie took a seat on the curb. The doors were glass so Alex was able to keep an eye on Allie. Meanwhile Alex walked over to Eve and began to figure out what the deal was with Eric.

"You work with her. What's up with this Eric character?" Alex asked Eve.

"I think Eric is her ex from Greenville. They were together for a long time, but recently Allie has come to realize how bad he has been treating her." Allie had just opened up to Eve earlier that day, which had given her more insight into Allie's troubled past. "She ended up dumping him right before coming to work here. He's really possessive over her. He's bad news Alex. She wanted to be here this summer to get away from him, and find herself again. I don't think it's a good idea for

Summer at The Point

them to talk. I'm not sure if she is strong enough yet, to turn him away. I don't think it has been enough time. We need to get closer and see what is going on." Eve thought a lot of Allie and she was trying to look out for her.

"Should I go out there?" Alex asked.

"No, Let me." Eve walked toward the entrance and noticed Eric had a tight grip on Allie's right wrist. It didn't alarm her until she noticed tears building up in Allie's eyes. Eve pushed the door open like she was about the fight Eric. "Let her go jackass." Eve pushed Eric.

"Look lady, this is none of your business." Eric began to talk back to Eve. Before anyone could stop him, Eric took out his pocketknife and swung it at Allie.

"Ahhhh!" Allie jumped back screaming. "Are you crazy? You cut my shirt." Allie put her hand on her chest and noticed blood. "Holy sh.... And me. You cut me." It was so fast, she didn't even feel any pain.

"It's thin babe. You should have backed away faster. I was just trying to scare you. I didn't really want to... I, um." Eric had lost his temper and was now trying to make excuses for his rash behavior.

"LEAVE!" Allie screamed as she clutched her chest.

Eric got in his car and squalled tires as he left the parking lot.

"Do you want me to call the police? Or your parents?" Eve reached for her cell phone.

"No. It's not a big cut. I didn't even feel it right away. Let's go back inside so I can get cleaned up. I have another shirt in my locker. I need to go change. I want to pretend like it didn't happen. No one else needs to know what happened." Allie walked briskly back into the restaurant. She didn't look at anyone as she made her way to the employee locker room. Some staff members were in the back getting ready for the contest, but she didn't pay them any attention even though she overheard the voices as people discussed the blood on her shirt. Allie opened her locker and went into one of the stalls. She undressed and assessed the cut. It mimicked a paper cut in width and was about two inches long. It was a thin cut that had already stopped bleeding. Allie took two bandages out of her bag and applied them before changing her shirt. She knew she had to deal with what just happened, but right now, she didn't have time. Allie had work to do and she was tired of letting her past dictate her future. Allie was now confident that coming here was definitely the right thing to do. She walked back out into the restaurant as if nothing had happened. Only a few of the guests had seen the event and she hoped nothing would come of it.

"Are you okay? Did you call the cops? He better not come back here." Alex was a little frantic and his testosterone had him fired up.

"Alex! It's okay. He's gone. I'm fine. No cops. Breathe!" Allie didn't know why, but she put her arms around Alex and hugged him not wanting to let go. "Thank you for being there for me." As Allie pulled away, it hit her, she really was falling for Alex. She didn't care how old he was or wasn't. He was stealing her heart. "I have to get back to work. I'll explain more about Eric later it you want me to." She grinned at Alex and turned back to finish her work. Allie grabbed her chest, but this time it had nothing to do with the cut. Instead, she was feeling her excited heart.

Eve approached Allie from behind. Since the boss was around, they had to appear as if they were working without distraction. "Are you okay?"

Allie didn't stop what she was doing, but she assured Eve that she would be fine. "Don't let anyone know details." Allie replied. "I know that people will talk, but only a few saw it. I'll be just fine." Allie noticed time was passing pretty quickly and it was already six thirty. The dinner crowd and ticket holders were steadily filing in. Allie wondered were Skyler was, and she was hoping that tonight would be less dramatic than the afternoon. Allie tied on her apron and began seating guests and taking drink orders.

CHAPTER ELEVEN

"Here she comes!" Braxton exclaimed as he watched Skyler coming down the steps. "Looking cute little lady!" Braxton had decided he would go back to acting as if he and Skyler were just friends. "Ready to kick some butt tonight?"

"Ha! I guess I'm as ready as I'm going to get." Skyler had already dressed for her performance, but she was having second thoughts about singing. She was doing an 80's rock song that she had been rehearsing for weeks. Skyler was dressed in black leather pants and hot pink shirt that was ripped showing a black tank top underneath. Her high heels made her nearly a foot taller than Braxton. "I'm bringing a change of clothes for our duet. Not sure, this look would work with our song. Let's roll buddy."

They did not talk about the drama that had taken place earlier that morning. Instead, they joked about all of the performers from last year, and they hoped the humiliation this year would be just as memorable.

It was six-thirty and the first performer would be taking the stage at seven. This year more people than ever had signed up to perform. There were forty-five contestants that would participate. Since it was a special event, the stage and buffet had been moved to the first floor. The plan was to have an all you can eat available up until eleven o'clock and the bar would serve until one.

Skyler and Braxton came into the front door and began looking around for a place to sit. It was already packed and contestants were checking in at a table by the elevators. The two decided to walk over and take a number.

"Hey Skyler. Here to sign in?" DJ was working the table.

"Hey DJ!." Skyler replied. "Oh, this is Braxton Davis. We'll be performing a duet tonight as well as our solos. So what are you doing working up here?"

"They needed some extra bodies around here tonight since some of the staff signed up to perform. Skyler, here is your number." DJ pinned the paper to Skyler's back. "And Braxton. Here you go."

"Have you seen Allie?" Skyler asked DJ.

"Yeah, she's working the dinner tables until ten, I think. You probably need to make a point to talk to her later. A big scene went down early between her and her ex Eric. I think she's okay, but she wouldn't say much to me or anyone else for that matter." DJ wanted to let Skyler know about the situation in hopes she could help Allie take her mind off what happened earlier today.

"Do you know if Alex is working?" Braxton chimed in.

"He's in the kitchen. He is doing his job, and covering for the manager from second. I think his name is Billy. Yeah, he was supposed to work, but he decided to sing, and Alex offered to fill in. He gets off at eleven. I think that's what I heard him tell Allie earlier." DJ finished her sentence while pinning on Braxton's number. "Well, looks like the crowd is getting restless." DJ finished with Skyler and look past her to the next person in line. "Good luck guys."

Skyler spotted a tall table by the window, so they made their way through the crowd to take a seat.

Only five minutes before the contest was scheduled to start. Contestants were still signing in and girls were still running in and out of the bathrooms making sure their hair and costumes were appropriate. Skyler scanned the crowd looking for Veronica, and other regular

Summer at The Point

performers. She noticed a table about three quarters of the way back where Bobby was seated with Katy and Sarah. Next to them Veronica, Marcy, and the rest of their snobby friends. Skyler caught herself starring. Once she made eye contact with Bobby, she quickly shook her head, and turned her attention to the stage. She noticed Mr. Davis walking up to the microphone signaling the show was about to begin.

"Welcome everybody, to the Rock Springs Annual Karaoke Contest. As you all know, this contest is not only based on how well our judges feel the contestants sing the songs, but also they are judging all other aspects of the performance. We will be looking at dance moves, fashion, and also crowd arousal. My name is Ron Davis and I will be the host for this year's contest. Let me start by introducing you to the judges who are seated over to my left. First, I would like to welcome, for the third year in a row, Mrs. Leslie Ferguson. Mrs. Ferguson and her husband are shareowners of the resort. She is an advertising executive from Southern California where she has lived for the past thirty-two years. Mrs. Ferguson was born just fifteen miles from here, and her parents were part of the group who founded this resort forty years ago. Her husband, John, and daughter, Diane, are in the audience tonight. To her right is Mr. James Pratt. Mr. Pratt is the owner of the grocery store down the street. I'm sure you all recognize him, and have often enjoyed one of his famous cheese biscuits. This is his first year judging the contest and we are pleased to have him here with us tonight. Welcome Mr. Pratt. Our final judge has been involved in this contest since it was first started. Dexter Callahan. Mr. Callahan is also a shareowner of the resort. He and his wife, Missy, are pharmaceutical sales representatives currently working for a company in Raleigh. Their daughter, Katy, is also out in the audience tonight. Welcome back Mr. Callahan. Okay, so let's get started. Kicking things off tonight will be one of our regular performers. Miss Marcy, are you ready?"

Mr. Davis left the stage, and the contest began. It was obvious who the favorites were, and it seemed one of them would claim this years prize. Marcy took the stage performing one of Britney Spears's songs. Sarah chose to go country and Veronica went with a classic rock ballad. DJ's crush, Mike Carmichael, was impressive and despite his uptight demeanor, he was quite a performer. The time finally came for Skyler to take the stage, and according to crowd chatter that Allie overheard, she was better this year than she has ever been. Skyler was definitely a crowd favorite.

"What a rush!" Skyler proclaimed as she ran up to Allie after her song. "I have to change clothes and sing again with Braxton this time."

"You were great." Allie remarked as she continued to work. She was happy for Skyler, but she had a lot on her mind. She was just trying to stay busy and not focus on what was going on around her.

"Braxton and I are the last act." Skyler was hoping Allie would snap out of her funk when she said, "I'm going to sing naked."

Allie turned her head and looked shockingly at Skyler. "Huh?"

"Ah, she's back. Are you okay?" Skyler asked. "You seem a bit distracted."

"I'm fine. I just want to get everything done so I can finish up by ten. I'll fill you in once I'm finished." Allie obviously wasn't herself, but she tried her best to convince Skyler that she was okay. Allie looked up and said, "Good luck with your duet. And try to keep your clothes on." Allie smiled at Skyler and then quickly got back to work.

Allie began to wonder if it was really fair for certain contestants to sing twice, but so many were doing it that it didn't seem to matter. While Skyler was changing, Veronica, Marcy, Sarah, and two other girls took the stage to do an old girl band routine. Allie hated that Skyler was missing this terrible presentation. Allie figured that Katy would have been in the group if her dad were not a judge.

After Skyler was dressed, she came back to join Braxton at their table. She noticed that Marcy and Veronica had taken the table next to them, making her apprehensive about approaching them. However, Braxton waived her over, so she put her issues aside.

"It's about time. Thought you had bailed on me." Braxton mentioned.

"Just wanted to go ahead and change for our act. Did I miss anything?" Skyler slid the chair back from the table and took a seat.

"Just more dumb girls singing dumb girl songs. The 'brat pack' just finished their group number." Braxton told her as he motioned over to Veronica and the girls.

"So in other words I didn't miss anything." Skyler chuckled. "Hey who's that guy? He looks familiar, sort of?" Skyler asked Braxton.

"Oh, that's Billy. He's the second floor manager. I guess he's next." Braxton could look at Skyler's face and tell she found Billy attractive. "He's not like us. Real country boy, you know?" Braxton was hoping Skyler would not develop a crush on Billy.

"Next up is one of our staff members. Billy, let's hear what you've got." Mr. Davis backed behind the curtain after announcing Billy.

As Billy took the stage, the lights faded down. He was wearing a worn out cowboy hat, snug jeans, and a button-up western shirt. He was holding a guitar as a prop as he sat on a stool in front of the microphone. Slow country music began to play and Billy belted out a classic that perfectly suited his deep southern voice. His eyes were focused in on a spot the crowd as if he visualized himself singing to someone. As he sang, Skyler found herself moving closer and closer to the stage as if he was hypnotizing her with his voice. His song of lost love and heartbreak really struck a cord with Skyler. She usually didn't like country music, but she connected emotionally with the song. When the song ended, Skyler applauded as if she was requesting an encore. The rest of the crowd seemed to enjoy it as well, and with that performance, Billy had become a front-runner in the competition. Once Skyler realized her dad was in the crowd glaring at her, she quickly went back to her seat.

"Wasn't he wonderful?" A love-struck Skyler asked Braxton. "He'll win for sure. I have to meet him."

It killed Braxton to say it, but he wanted to make Skyler happy. Braxton could see it in Skyler's eyes. She was definitely attracted to Billy. Braxton would rather have Skyler as a friend than not have her at all. So, he surprised himself when he offered to introduce her to him. "I can introduce you to him, if you want." Braxton secretly hoped Skyler would say no.

"You are really good at the friend thing." Skyler was surprised. "I underestimated you." Skyler kissed Braxton's cheek with gratitude.

It was a quarter after eight when Mr. Davis allowed time for a short fifteen-minute intermission. They had reached the halfway point.

Braxton noticed Billy over by the bar. He was talking with the new bartender, Lane, and appeared to be ordering a beer. Braxton figured this was as good of time as any to introduce him to Skyler. "Ready to meet him? I'm surprised you don't know him. He was here last summer." Braxton mentioned as they walked over. "He even bowled with Alex."

"I was a little preoccupied with Bobby last summer. Remember?" Skyler reminded Braxton.

"Ah, but you always had time for me." Braxton gave her a half smile and a flirty wink.

Skyler ruffled Braxton's hair in response to his flirtation. Then she looked over at Billy and noticed Marcy was already throwing herself at him. "Maybe now isn't the time."

Realizing why Skyler was apprehensive, Braxton grabbed her hand and assured her, "He's not into Marcy. You know better than anyone how she is. She's a leech. Let's go." Skyler was trying to back out, but Braxton pulled her along.

"Hey man! You rocked it dude." Braxton complimented Billy.

"Thanks Braxton." Billy thanked Braxton as he patted him on the back. He then focused his attention on Skyler. "I'm Billy." Billy reached out his hand to shake the palm of a nervous Skyler. Billy was nervous too. This was

Summer at The Point

the chance he had been waiting for. Even though he still had the adrenaline pumping, he attempted to remain calm and to keep it together.

"Skyler." That was all she could say as she shook his hand. Once she realized she was blushing, she quickly pulled her hand away.

"Want to join us?" We have a table up towards the front." Braxton offered Billy. He ignored Marcy as she continued trying to latch on to Billy.

"Sure." Marcy remarked.

"Not you Marcy. You can go back with your friends." Braxton gently pushed Marcy aside. "Billy, what do you say?" Braxton had no intentions of sitting with Marcy. He was still annoyed with the way she had acted earlier that morning.

"Is it okay with you?" Billy politely asked Skyler. Not paying any mind to Marcy, he stepped forward and tilted Skyler's chin up so that he could she her eyes.

"Of course." Skyler replied in a gentle voice. She then reached to grab his hand, and guided him back to her table.

Skyler, Braxton, and Billy returned to their table leaving Marcy behind to pout. Allie was watching the interaction from across the room. The expression on Marcy's face made her grin. She loved watching someone be told no, when they were so used to getting everything they wanted. Cruel, maybe she thought, but entertaining nonetheless. Allie was glad Billy and Skyler had finally met. She new something good would come from their union. Allie was also surprised at how well Braxton was handling everything. It was obvious he thought a lot of Skyler. It's rare to find a man who doesn't let jealousy get the best of him. Braxton definitely impressed Allie with the way he handled himself.

"Show's almost done girly. You'll be joining them soon, I assume?" Eve caught Allie watching Skyler and Braxton.

Allie was beginning to see Eve as family. Her friendship and wisdom were well appreciated as Allie adjusted to being away from home. "I guess I will, at least for a little while. You were right about this karaoke thing. It's a lot of fun and the tips are pretty good too. We should do these events more often."

"There's a pageant at the end of the summer, tips aren't bad for that either." Eve mentioned.

"Good. That should be fun." Allie replied as she bussed off a dirty table.

Eve grabbed the dirty glasses to help Allie. "I wanted to let you know, that some weekends I have Skyler, Braxton, and some of the others over to eat a real home cooked meal and spend the night. If you ever want to join us, you are welcome to. It's nice to have a break from this place every now and then, especially when you miss home." Eve and Allie had really begun to bond. It was nice for each of them to have someone to talk to.

"I'd love to do that some time." Allie smiled at Eve as she grabbed the water pitcher and went to offer refills. She wanted to ask Eve if Alex stayed too, but she figured he does since Eve was his family.

******

Allie clocked out at ten since another waitress was coming in to close. She could have stayed and received more tips, but she was ready to call it a night. She decided to join Billy at the table to watch Skyler and Braxton perform. There was only one more act ahead of them so they were already preparing backstage. "So you two finally met? How do you think it's going?" Allie asked Billy.

"She is even more wonderful than I imagined. I think she might actually like me. She keeps giggling and smiling at me. Seems surreal." Billy grinned and adjusted to toothpick in his mouth.

"I figured she would be into you. She needs someone like you. I am glad that it's working out so far. Have ya'll made any plans for later?" Allie knew Skyler would want to hang out until late tonight and she wondered if she had invited Billy to The Point.

"She hasn't brought up anything. Maybe I should?" Billy suggested.

"I'd wait, and let her make the plans, I'm sure she'll suggest something." Allie replied.

The color of the lights changed to a bright red as Mr. Davis took the stage to announce the last performers.

"Closing out the contest are two of last years favorites. Let's give it up for Braxton and Skyler." Mr. Davis announced as his son took the stage with Skyler.

Braxton and Skyler came out onto the stage jumping and waving their arms in the air trying to get the crowd involved. They sang a rap duet that was a big hit from a few summers back. They were so energetic and entertaining, it was the perfect finale.

There was going to be a twenty-minute break while the judges tallied up the scores and announced the winner. Skyler decided to go make one last wardrobe change before the judges announced their decision. Allie knew all of the bathrooms were still full of contestants and their props, so she suggested Skyler use the employee locker room. The girls excused themselves and headed toward the back of the restaurant.

"Should we go out to The Point tonight?" Skyler asked Allie from behind the stall.

"I think that would be a great idea. Are you going to

invite Billy?" Allie hoped that was what Skyler was planning.

"Yeah. I thought it would be a good chance for us to get to know each other, and for you to tell me about what happened today with Eric? Are you okay?" Skyler hoped that her friend was doing alright, and that Eric did not mess with her head too badly.

Allie didn't like that someone had already mentioned the situation to Skyler. She should have known by the way the resort people gossiped that it wouldn't be long before everyone knew. "I'll be fine. Seeing Eric made me realize that I am better off without him. Alex and Eve were both here when Eric showed up. I have a lot to explain to them, but I will worry about it later. I'm hoping to get a chance to talk to Alex about it tonight." Allie was hinting to Skyler that she did want to go to The Point, and that she wanted Alex to be there too.

"We'll head out there after they announce the winner. It is nearly eleven and Alex should be off soon. I'll invite everyone and we can pile in my golf cart. I drove the red one and it can seat six." Skyler put her arm around Allie's shoulders and said, "Let's head back out there girl. And just so you know, I'm here to listen if you need me."

"Thanks." Allie knew she could trust Skyler, but for some reason the only person she wanted to talk to was Alex. She wanted to explain about her volatile relationship with Eric, and she hoped that it wouldn't scare Alex away from her.

"Well folks the time was come to announce the winner. Contestants gather around the stage." Mr. Davis attempted to gain the crowd's attention.

Allie noticed Alex was up by the server station talking to Eve and they were both looking her way. Allie smiled and waived at Eve as Alex began to walk towards her. "Mind if I sit." Alex asked.

"Sure you can sit. They are about to announce the winner." Allie replied.

Alex pulled the chair up close to hers so that they were both facing the stage. "I think our buddy Skyler has a pretty good chance at winning." Alex said as he placed his hand on Allie's knee.

"Yeah, I think so too. She was really good, I had no idea she could sing that well." Allie responded nervously.

Mrs. Ferguson got up from her seat, walked a sealed envelope up to the stage, and handed it to Mr. Davis.

"Okay. In third place this year we have Miss Veronica." Mr. Davis handed her a bouquet. Veronica looked disgusted that she did not win.

"Second place this year will be Miss Skyler Richardson." Mr. Davis gave her a bouquet as well. Skyler wondered who could have gotten first place if she and Veronica

Summer at The Point

were just the runners-up.

Now that the lights were low, Skyler was able to look out into the audience to find her dad, but to her dismay, he had already left the restaurant. She hoped he had at least stayed long enough to hear both of her performances. Skyler was happy she did well, but saddened that she was unable to show her gift to her dad.

"Wahoo!" Allie hollered. She noticed a smirk on Veronica's face that showed she was happy Skyler did not win. "It's sad when people get pleasure from other people's shortcomings." She thought.

"And this year's Karaoke Champion is Mr. Billy Douglas. Come claim your prize!" Billy walked across the stage and stood in front of Mr. Davis. Mr. Davis handed Billy his check and all of the females in the crowd screamed and cheered to show their support.

"Skyler's blushing a little. She likes him, doesn't she?" Alex asked Allie referring to Billy.

"I suppose." Allie did not want to say much. It was pretty obvious considering Skyler was nearly drooling as she fixated her stare on Billy.

"Well, he said he wanted to impress her, and it looks like he succeeded." Alex offered his opinion.

"Yeah, looks like you're right." Allie said as she watched Skyler push through a crowd of teenage girls to give

Billy a congratulation hug.

"You'll be joining us tonight I hope." Skyler asked Billy.

"Sure, I can hang out for a while tonight. What's the plan?" Billy questioned.

"We were going to go out to 'The Point.'" Skyler responded.

"Yeah, okay. That sounds like fun." Billy replied as a couple of twenty-something year old female fans jumped on his back while holding a bottle of champagne nearly pulling him to the ground.

Skyler couldn't help but laugh. "I'll meet you out front in a few. I'm on the long red golf cart." She turned to walk away.

"How about a little help?" Billy asked as he picked the girls off one by one.

"I think you've got it covered cowboy." Skyler grinned and went to find Alex. Maybe he could help calm the crowd.

CHAPTER TWELVE

For once, Braxton felt out of place, and like a fifth wheel as they headed out to The Point. Skyler was driving, and Billy was sitting next to her. Allie was in the middle row with Alex and Braxton was on the back alone. Braxton knew that Alex liked Allie and Skyler was crazy over Billy, so he wondered why he even bothered to go.

"You can let me off at my cabin. I'm going to get my dad's golf cart and head out to see Josh." Braxton told Skyler.

"Are you sure?" Skyler asked, not trying to talk him out of it.

"Yeah. I'll go get him and then we'll come down there." Braxton replied.

"Okay." Skyler pulled into the drive. "See you in a little bit then. " Skyler drove off a little concerned that Braxton was bailing on them, but happy that Billy was with her.

They were the first to arrive at The Point, and since the bar was still open, the crowd continued to celebrate up at the restaurant.

Once they parked, Skyler immediately stripped down to her bikini, ran down to the rocks, and jumped in. "Come on Billy!"

Billy responded by imitating her, and dove off the rocks into the deep water.

"We can sit for a while if you want?" Alex offered his hand to pull Allie off the golf cart.

"Okay. Want to sit over there?" Allie pointed at the large rock furthest from the golf cart. They held hands as they went to take a seat.

"So do you want to talk about what happened today with Eric?" Alex hoped Allie would really open up to him.

"I suppose I should. Just let me ramble, and I will eventually get through it." Allie took a deep breath before continuing with her story. "Here it goes. Eric and

I met about four years ago. I thought he was special because he was older and everyone knew of him. I thought being with him would make me feel better about myself. But being with him slowly made me hate myself. At first things were great, he acted like he really cared about me. We were always together. We were nearly inseparable. Then he began to insult me, and try to change me. He would embarrass me in public, and make me feel like a fool. He made me dress a certain way. He would make me spend all of my money on new clothes that I did not even like. He would give me haircuts and dye my hair nearly ever week. I hated how I looked. I never wanted to leave the house. He crushed my confidence to assure that I would never leave him. When I went to college, I thought things would be better, and I would be able to break away from him. Then he started demanding I come home every weekend to see him. If I didn't, he would come to my apartment. Eventually the more I tried to refuse, the more severe the punishment. He always kept a pocket knife on him, and if I didn't cooperate, well..." Allie began to cry, but she knew she needed to finish the story. Alex put is arm around her and pulled her close.

"He started cutting me. They were always small cuts where no one could see. But I felt so disfigured and became severely depressed. That is when I stopped eating. I actually ended up becoming hospitalized with malnutrition and dehydration. I knew that was my chance to be free of him. I wanted to let the doctors know what was really going on, but I could not. I was scared." Allie began to feel very vulnerable at this moment, but she took comfort in knowing that Alex was there for her.

"After two weeks in the hospital, I returned to college and had a lot of work to catch up on. My mom was worried about me, so she came and stayed with me for nearly a month after that. Surprisingly, Eric did not come around during that time, and I was able to start turning things around. It was nearly time for summer break when my mom returned home. But before she left, she found out about this job. I called up Mr. Davis right away and asked about the interview process. Before I knew it, I had a job. More importantly, I knew Eric could not get to me if I was here. So, I packed my bags, wrote Eric a letter. I attempted to call him, but I could never reach him, so I just took the letter to his mom. I asked her to give it to him, and then I came straight here. Except for today, I hadn't seen him since right before I was hospitalized." Allie dropped her head and avoided eye contact with Alex. "While I was in the hospital, I was able to talk with a psychiatrist each day in a private session. Other than her, I have not been able to talk about this with anyone else. I didn't even tell my mom all of the details. She just thought that I was stressed and depressed about college and fitting in, and that I just stopped eating and began over-exercising. You know, being here is really helping me, other than today, I have not even thought about Eric. I've always thought that everything happens for a

Summer at The Point

reason, and I feel like this job, this resort, and well... you, were introduced into my life for a reason." Allie had stopped crying, but her face was red and her eyes swollen. "Please don't change the way you see me." She wiped her face, and she noticed that Alex still had his arm around her shoulders.

"That's a lot for a person to have to deal with. I don't think that it is something you get over in just a few weeks or months. That is something you will always remember and learn from." Alex comforted her with his understanding point of view. "I want you to know that if you ever feel like you need to vent about it or cry over it, I am going to be here for you. I am not trying to put any pressure on you about a relationship. I just want you to know that I think you are great, and I am not going anywhere. You do not deserve to be treated the way Eric treated you. You're special Allie, and you need to know that." Alex offered a lot of wisdom for such a young person. He took his arm off Allie's shoulder and grabbed her hands, pulling her around to face him. "I'll help you get past it. Let's spend the rest of this summer having fun and hanging out. Just like Skyler vowed to do at the start of the summer. I can help you take your mind off Eric." Alex put his hand on Allie's chin and lifted her face. "You know Allie, you have got some pretty eyes." Alex starred at Allie, he wanted to kiss her, but didn't want to scare her away.

"Alex, thank you for listening to me." Allie responded as she offered a crooked smile.

Allie leaned in and kissed Alex. Tears of mixed emotions ran down her face. So many thoughts raced through Allie's mind. In those few moments, she realized that Alex was amazing, and he was exactly the type of person that she wanted to be with. He was kind, cute, and hardworking. She admired Alex, and she looked forward to getting to know him better. She was done with Eric, and meeting Alex made her realize that there was someone else out there who could care about her the way she wanted to be cared for.

"Are you okay?" Alex backed away and wiped a tear from Allie's cheek. "I didn't mean to upset you."

"You didn't, I'm fine. I just have a lot on my mind. Today has been pretty crazy and I'm sorry for being so emotional." Allie was embarrassed that she let herself breakdown in front of Alex. "Looks like Skyler and Billy are really hitting it off." Allie pointed towards them as she changed the subject.

Allie caught herself watching Skyler and Billy, not meaning to stare, she was just incredibly happy for both of them. Skyler was laughing, smiling, and kissing Billy as if she was truly mesmerized by him. It seemed perfect, it seemed natural. "Hey guys, are ya'll going to get in?" Skyler asked from the water.

Alex and Allie exchanged looks as the thought about whether or not they wanted to get in.

"You can if you want. I think I'm just going to go back

to my room though. I'm not really myself tonight." Allie spoke to Alex as she realized that it would probably be best if she pulled away from the group, and walked back to the cabin. She contemplated asking Alex to walk with her, but she couldn't get up the nerve to ask him. Allie stood up, walked to the end of the rocks, and shouted out to Skyler. "I think I'm going to call it a night. I'll find you tomorrow. Have fun."

"Are you sure?" Skyler didn't want Allie to leave. She knew that she had a hard day and she wanted to make sure she was alright. "Do you need me to walk with you, or take you on the golf cart?"

"I'm going to walk with her." Alex replied before Allie could say anything otherwise. "I'll make sure she gets back okay. I'll catch you guys tomorrow."

"Okay guys. We'll see ya'll tomorrow." Skyler called out.

"Later Alex. Night Allie." Billy said bye and quickly turned his attention back to Skyler. "Okay sweetheart, so what are you thinking?"

"I'm thinking that I wish I had met you last year. I'm thinking that you are really handsome, and a great singer. What are you thinking?" Skyler couldn't take her eyes off Billy. She wasn't looking for love, but she felt like she might have stumbled across it anyway.

"I'm thinking that I can't believe how lucky I am to be here with you. I knew the first time I saw you, that you were awesome. I am so glad we finally got a chance to meet." Billy kissed Skyler's smile. They both knew that something was going to come from this relationship, it was the beginning of the real deal.

Meanwhile, Allie and Alex were making the long walk back to the employee cabins. There was an awkward silence Allie wanted to continue to open up to Alex, but she didn't want to get hurt again. Even though his age was not a big deal to Allie, it did mean that he was more likely to bail on her when she needed him most. Even if he was making promises to stand by her and be there for her, Allie wondered if he was being sincere. Someone once told her that to find happiness you had to be willing to take chances and live your life. Allie didn't love Eric. She pondered if she even knew what love was. Then she shook her head angry at herself for even thinking about love. She barely knew Alex or his intentions. Once they got to the next bend in the path, Allie stopped and looked Alex in the eyes. "Would you ever break my heart?" She asked him, not knowing why, out of all the thoughts in her head, that question leaked out.

"Oh course not. Not on purpose. Are you still questioning what we talked about?" Alex grabbed Allie's hands.

"It's just that I really like you, and I have since the first time I saw you. I just cannot handle being hurt again. I am just so fragile right now. I would love for us to spend more time together, and take things slow. I mean, if you

113

want to." Allie was trying to make Alex see where she was coming from, and she hoped he would understand.

"How about we start off by watching a movie together? We can go to Braxton's cabin. I want to spend time with you too." Alex just wanted to be near Allie, and take her mind off of everything. He knew that if they just hung out that she would warm up to him and forget about all the negative things she had dealt with in the past.

"I've got a few horror flicks at the cabin. DJ is going to be out tonight, if you want to watch a movie in my dorm. I've got popcorn too." Allie smiled and pulled Alex's hand as they started back walking.

"That sounds good." Alex squeezed Allie's hand, and followed her toward the employee cabin. "I wonder how late Skyler and Billy are planning on staying out. It looked like they really hit it off. You know, the four of us should stay off resort with Eve some time. It would be a good break for you I think."

"Yeah, I think that would fun. Are you sure that would be okay with Eve?" Allie inquired even though she already knew the answer.

"It was actually her idea. She suggested it a few weeks ago, except she mentioned Braxton." Alex knew that Eve would be fine with substituting Billy for Braxton.

They arrived at the employee housing, and made their way past the crowd of drunken employees scattered around the main entrance. Allie was somewhat embarrassed by the appearance of DJ's side of the room, but she didn't think Alex would mind. They pushed all of the furniture against the back wall, and threw pillows, blankets, and a sleeping bag on the floor. Allie popped popcorn while Alex put in the DVD. The two sat down and enjoyed a quiet movie night together. They stayed up all night talking and watching nearly every movie Allie had brought from home. Allie couldn't have asked for a better night with a better guy. Once she felt comfortable, Allie laid her head in Alex's lap. He ran his fingers through her hair and watched her face glow from the reflection of the television. She was beautiful, he thought, just like a picture. Alex figured he could stay like this forever.

The night flew by quickly and the morning sun would be rising shortly. Allie decided to crawl into bed and get some sleep. Especially since Alex was already snoring on the floor. She giggled quietly as she pulled herself off the floor and fell back onto her bed. She hoped to get a few hours of sleep before embarking on a new day.

Summer at The Point

CHAPTER THIRTEEN

"What the heck?" DJ was surprised when she returned to her room and saw Alex asleep on the floor. It was six-thirty and she was coming back to get ready for her shift at the pool. "Well, hello there Alex. You two must have stayed up late."

"Hey." Alex mumbled.

"All night to be exact. Sorry about the mess girl." Allie sat up in her bed, exhausted and speaking in her sleepy voice. "What time is it?"

"Six-thirty. Don't worry about the mess. I'm headed out again. Got to be at the pool by seven." DJ grabbed her bathing suit and went into the bathroom to change. "I'll help straighten up later. Most of the mess is mine anyway." DJ made a quick change, and headed out the door. "I'll see you later."

"I really don't want to get up. Oh, wow, I'm tired." Allie said as a squirmed in her bed and pulled the covers back over her head.

"I guess I need to get to Braxton's to shower and change clothes." Alex sat up and pulled himself up off the floor. "I had a good time." He started folding the blankets and putting them away. "Do you work tonight?"

"Yeah, I have to go in from four until ten o'clock. I'm glad we got to hang out." Allie was still unsure about Alex and his intention. "I'll catch up with you later. I'm going to sleep a little more, and then go find Skyler before I go to work."

Alex put on his cap, and headed toward the door. "Yeah, I might try to find Billy and see how everything went after we split. I'll find you after work. I get off at eleven." Alex hugged Allie and kissed her cheek. As he was shutting the door, he winked at her one last time before starting his day.

"Hmm... he's such a nice guy." Allie said out loud to herself as she pulled the covers back over her head.

Allie was able to doze off briefly, but awoke soon after

to a loud knock at the door.

"Knock, Knock, is anyone in there. Allie? DJ? Hello." A voice was screaming from outside Allie's door.

Allie pulled her self out of the bed and mumbled a frustrated, "I'm coming."

"It's about time. I've been out here for like ten minutes. Were you still asleep?" Skyler was extremely bubbly and high-spirited this morning.

"I was up all night watching movies. I was going to try and get some sleep before going into work." Allie offered excuses for her tired, lazy appearance.

"Well, it's nearly one o'clock. You need to get moving. I have lots to talk about with you." Skyler busted in the door and slammed it behind herself. "What did you do to the furniture? Did Alex stay here last night?"

"He stayed and slept on the floor. It was just so late when we finished watching my movies, he crashed here instead of walking to Braxton's alone." Allie was talking fast as if she was trying to make excuses.

"You don't have to explain anything to me. I'm glad he stayed." Skyler replied.

"We had a good time, and I was able to get to know him a little better." Allie smiled as she thought about Alex.

118

"Oh, that is too cute. I'm glad you two are hitting it off. He needs someone in his life with some direction." Skyler thought it was time to let her friend know about some of the bad habits that Alex has had in the past. "I know he thinks a lot of you."

"Some direction?" Allie wondered what Skyler meant by that statement. "What do you mean?"

"Alex is pretty gullible and can easily be steered the wrong way. Some of his old friends including Marcy are real losers and can have a bad influence on him. I think if he's with you, then he won't be tempted to hang out with them." Skyler didn't want Allie to get hurt after she had already been through so much with Eric. "I wanted to tell you about it earlier, but I wanted you to see how you felt about him first. He really is a great guy, he's just made some poor choices in the past." Skyler offered this heads up to Allie in hopes she would be prepared for whatever situations that might arise.

Allie was not expecting Skyler to tell her about Alex's flaws, but these were things she needed to know. After all, she was interested in learning everything about him. She wondered who some of these friends of his were, and why Skyler had not mentioned them before. After all, Skyler has always talked about how down to earth and caring Alex was. It was hard to imagine him being any different than that. "Everyone has a past and everyone has flaws. I'm not planning on getting too close to Alex right now, anyway. I know better than to let my guard down too soon. I just want to get to know

119

him better. Thank you for letting me know this, but I don't think I have to worry about him. He seems pretty headstrong, at least when he talks to me." Allie hoped that Alex was sincere with her about who he was. She didn't think she could handle another guy like Eric.

"And that is what I'm counting on, I hope he continues to be the good Alex for you. I just felt like after everything that went on yesterday, well, I just don't want you to rebound to Alex and get hurt again by letting your guard down too soon. He is a good guy, but you still need to be cautious. Us girls have to look after one another, you know." Skyler plopped down on DJ's bed.

"You're right. So speaking of looking out for each other. How was your night?" Allie cheesed a grin Skyler's way.

"Ah, well. It was amazing, incredible, outstanding, and magical." Skyler was beaming. She had never been with a guy that made her feel the way Billy did. He was actually able to take her mind off her fling with Braxton. At least for now, she was content with being Billy's girl, even if her past with Braxton always had a way of resurfacing.

"That good, huh? Wow! Look's like some one is falling head over heels pretty quickly." Allie was happy for Skyler. Billy was definitely an improvement from Bobby, and even though his looks weren't quite as impressive as Braxton's, he was still an all-around better catch out of the three.

"I want to spend every single day with Billy. I want to know all of his likes, dislikes, and quirks. And when he leaves the resort to manage his own restaurant, I want to follow him." Skyler seemed to be daydreaming about the life she felt she could have if she stayed with Billy.

"Wow, slow down girl. All of this after one night. You might want to get to know him better before you think of running off with him. I know you don't want to go through with the plans your dad mapped out, but I think you are being a little hasty here." Allie was caught off guard when Skyler made that comment. Allie's reply may have seemed inconsiderate and insincere, but she didn't want her friend to jump into something too quickly. Allie had concerns for Skyler and Billy's relationship, just as Skyler did for Allie and Alex's. "Plus, I know how close you were with Braxton, and all of this has pretty much changed overnight."

"I do still love Braxton, I always will. It's just with Braxton, it's never serious. I was cool with that at first, it was actually what I thought I wanted. But nothing is better than a guy holding you and telling you that you are his everything. Falling for someone is exciting. I had missed the rush of a first kiss and the late night cuddling. I think I need this thing with Billy. He's swept me off my feet and I'm loving it." Skyler was obviously love struck and not acting like the same girl Allie met at the start of the summer. "Billy believes that you have to take chances to find happiness, and he said singing in the karaoke

Summer at The Point

contest was his way of taking a chance of impressing me. He feels the same way I do Allie. He wants me to follow through with my goals, and not be afraid to take chances. He is already inspiring me so much."

"Whatever you want Skyler, I will support you. Just follow your own advice, and don't dive in too quickly. You can take chances, but you still need to be cautious of your actions." Allie got up and grabbed some clothes. She figured she would go ahead and shower since she was already up. "I guess I need to shower, and go eat something myself."

"Alright, well I'm going to go meet up with Billy. He has rented one of the pontoon boats, so I'm going to go help him gas it up. Since The Point will probably be crowded tonight, we thought the four of us could ride out to Fox Bend. It's a little island that's not to far from here. Do you think you and Alex could come?" Skyler wanted the four of them to start getting away from the rest of the resort crowd.

"I can ask Alex when I get to work. I think it would be fun. What time did you want to meet?" Allie thought it might be nice for them to get away, but, she wondered who Braxton would be hanging out with now, since Skyler was with Billy. Allie actually felt bad for Braxton, but he knew Braxton was used to this sort of 'relationship' with Skyler.

"Billy gets off around eleven. So, if you and Alex are off by then, maybe we can meet at the boat dock around eleven-thirty." Skyler was hoping Alex would agree to the arrangement.

"Okay. I get off at ten. I guess I can come back here to change and then meet you guys after that." Allie wanted to look nice for Alex, even if it was just a boat ride. She was already thinking about what she would wear. Skyler was right, there was something to be said about the magic of a first kiss and a new romance.

Skyler didn't want Allie to have to walk across the resort by herself so she figured she could give her a ride. "Well, I can pick you up at ten outside the restaurant, and I'll bring you back here to get ready. It will be faster that way."

"Okay. I'll see you at ten then." Allie shut the door behind Skyler and went to take a shower.

Allie was about to step into the shower when she once again heard voices coming from her neighbors room. They were the same voices from before when the room raiding incident occurred. Allie wanted to stop whatever it was they were doing, but instead she listened intently to see what they were scheming.

"It just makes me so angry. We got her away from Bobby. We lucked up with her losing interest in Braxton, but now she has Billy. I'm sick of her always ending up with the cute guy. Grab that lip gloss and those flip-flops." Veronica was stealing and plotting. She really was evil. "But that's alright because I have already implemented the perfect plan to mess up Skyler's little life."

"What is it Veronica?" It once again sounded like Marcy was Veronica's accomplice.

"Let's just say, once this plan delivers the expected outcome, her life is going to get slightly more complicated, and her parents won't be able to forgive this mix-up." Allie wished she knew what the mix-up was that Veronica was referring to. "And once we draft Alex back to our side, we will once again rule this resort."

"If you can get Alex back for me, I will owe you so big. I wish he would quit hanging around with that stupid waitress. He was mine first." Marcy was always whining.

"And he will be yours again. John is back now and he is going to help us with that. Once we get Alex back with his old crowd, he will forget about her." Veronica was always up to something and she figured her plan would be flawless. "Let's get out of here."

Allie waited for them to leave before she got into the shower. She was really beginning to worry about what she had overheard. It was funny that they mentioned John and Alex's 'old crowd.' Maybe that was what Skyler was hinting at. Maybe that was why Skyler wanted Allie and Alex off the resort tonight. Now Allie definitely thought that the pontoon ride was a good idea. She wondered if she should warn Skyler about what she had heard. Once again, she knew she should alert her roommate to what Veronica had taken, but she would have to find a way to do that without letting Veronica know she was on to her.

After her shower, Allie warmed up a microwaveable dinner, and phoned home to check in with her mother. Once Allie assured her mom that everything at the resort was going well, she straightened up the room, and left for the restaurant. She packed a change of clothes just in case Skyler arrived late to pick her up. Allie walked to the restaurant thinking about all she had overheard earlier. She was obviously concerned, but she tried to stay positive and have faith in Alex's character. After putting her things in her locker, Allie walked to the kitchen to speak with Alex before clocking in.

Allie stuck her head into the kitchen and tried to ignore the catcalls from the kitchen staff. "Hey Alex. Can I talk to you for a second?"

"What's up?" Alex asked as he adjusted the apron around his waist.

"Did you get a chance to talk to Billy?" Allie figured she would let Alex bring up tonight, hoping that he knew about the plan.

"Yeah, I told him we would go tonight. Is that okay with you?" Alex held Allie's hand as he asked. "I wasn't trying to answer for you. I just thought it would be good for us, and I didn't want to miss the opportunity."

"No, yeah, I mean, I do want to go. I had told Skyler yes too. Is it okay if you and Billy meet us at the boat dock after you get off? Skyler is going to pick me up so I can change." Allie didn't know if Alex had thought that far ahead.

"Yeah, he's meeting me outback after he closes up his floor. We'll meet you guys at the dock around eleven-fifteen." Alex pulled Allie toward him. "I'll see you then, okay?" He kissed her cheek and walked back toward the kitchen.

"Okay." Allie watched him go back to work and high five the sweaty guy who was cutting vegetables over by the sink. Allie sighed, and then went to clock in. She hoped the night would be steady so time would pass quickly.

******

"You heading out?" The new bartender, Lane, called out to Allie.

"Yeah. I made plans with a friend of mine." Allie replied. "What time do you get off?"

"Hopefully, I'll be out of here by one, but last night it was nearly three before I clocked out." Lane seemed like a nice girl, and if had been another night, Allie might have been more willing to hang around and chat. Lane was in school for interior design at a local college. She commutes to work since she only lives twenty minutes away from the resort. Lane was a tall, slender brunette who appeared to be at least five years older than Allie.

"Oh man, well have a good night. I'll see you later." Allie was anxious yet excited to get the night started. She ran out the door to meet Skyler.

Skyler had parked the golf cart on the curb. Her hair was in tight curls that were pushed back by a black headband. Skyler was already in her bikini and cut-off jean shorts. She was ready for the night's festivities.

"It's about time you got out here, it's nearly ten-thirty. Let's go get you ready." Skyler sped quickly across the resort so Allie would have time to change. The golf cart held up well as Skyler made hairpin turns at top speed.

"Sorry, I was talking to the new girl." Allie apologized for her tardiness. "Oh, by the way Skyler, I wanted to ask you something. Do you know of anyone on the resort named John? I don't know his last name." Allie figured Skyler would know who she was talking about.

"There is John Cohen. He's Marcy's older brother. Alex used to hang out with him all the time. John's bad news. How did you hear about him?" Skyler didn't want Allie to find out all of this from anyone else. That's why she wanted to take out the pontoon. She knew John

Summer at The Point

was back and she wanted to be the one to tell Allie.

"I heard some girls talking about him, and how he used to hang around with Alex. I think it was Veronica and Marcy. What's so bad about him?" Allie was interested to know what kind of people Alex used to associate with.

"John was kicked off the resort the last week of the season last year after they found drugs on his golf cart. Alex had been off the resort for about two weeks before that visiting his grandmother. I don't know if he knew that John did drugs. Earlier last summer however, he was caught breaking into Mr. Carmichael's condo, and Alex was apparently accused of being an accomplice. He nearly lost his job." Skyler was blunt as she educated Allie about John.

"Wow, so Alex did flirt with danger in the past, huh." Allie was concerned.

"I do know that Alex used to drink with him, but that was last summer. I don't think he's even seen him since. Oh, and I should mention that the same night he got kicked out, he also got in a fight with a few of the other male members. Mike Carmichael and Josh Holland messed him up pretty bad. They had to take him to the regional hospital." As they parked the golf cart and headed inside, Skyler explained how John was a total loser, and for a while, Alex was his right hand man. "Wait, where did you run into Veronica and Marcy?"

"They were snooping through my neighbor's room again, and I overheard them plotting. They want to take Billy away from you, and get Alex back in there little group so he can be with Marcy again. Same old drama." Allie knew Skyler was not afraid of whatever Veronica had planned, but she wanted Skyler to watch her back just the same.

"She's a pain, isn't she. I'm not going to let her get Billy away from me, and you should hold tight to Alex as well. She tries to rule the resort, and make everyone part of her little puppet show. Don't worry about it, I'm not." Skyler was used to Veronica and her little schemes.

"Great. I'm so over drama. Let's get the hell away from this place tonight." Allie stripped down and changed into something a little cuter. She chose to wear her black bikini topped with jean shorts and a purple spaghetti-strapped top.

"That's the plan." Skyler stole DJ's blanket off her bed. "Might need this, it will probably be pretty chilly out there tonight. Do you have another?"

Allie pulled out a box from under her bed. "Yeah, here's two more. Okay, I guess I'm ready. Let's get out of here. It's already ten minutes after eleven."

They hopped back on the golf cart and sped down to the boat dock. Billy was already sitting in the driver's seat, but where was Alex.

"Hey cutie." Billy said as he kissed Skyler.

"Where's Alex?" Skyler asked. She could see that Allie was getting nervous, especially since she had heard so much about John. Skyler hoped Alex hadn't backed out on them.

"Oh, he's just gone to get the cooler. He got off a little early, and I sent him back to my room to get a few things. There he is, he's got someone's golf cart. He had Braxton's earlier, I wonder who that one belongs to?" Billy said as he pointed up to the path.

Allie let out a sigh of relief, but she did wonder whose golf cart Alex had borrowed.

"Ya'll ready?" Alex asked as he loaded the cooler onto the boat along with a paper bag full of snacks. "I have to take this golf cart to The Point and drop it off. Billy want to ride with me. It will only take a second."

"Yeah, if the ladies don't mind waiting a few minutes. Let's hurry though, I'm ready to ride." Billy got off the boat and sat on the passenger's side as they took off. They didn't even give Allie or Skyler a chance to say whether they would mind or not.

"Well, that was odd." Skyler didn't like the shady behavior that Alex was exhibiting.

"Yeah, I'm not so sure how I'm feeling about this now. I want to trust Alex, but I'm starting to question whether or not that is a good idea." Allie had a sick feeling in her stomach. It was as if her intuition was letting her know that it was John's golf cart.

"Don't stress over it girl. It's all good, I'm sure." Skyler hoped it was all going to be okay. Her friend deserved to be happy.

It took about ten minutes for the boys to return on foot. Skyler didn't know why Billy didn't just follow Alex in her cart so they wouldn't have to walk back, but it was only a short distance.

"Alright, let's start it up Billy." Alex yelled out. "Hey pretty lady, is this seat taken?"

Allie noticed that Alex smelled of beer and seemed to be more talkative than normal. "Are you drunk?" All Allie could think was that Alex got off early and was drinking with John.

"He's fine. He just snuck a beer or two out of the cooler." Billy excused his friend.

Allie cut her eyes at Alex. She didn't know whether or not Billy was telling the truth. "Okay, well hand me one." She figured what the heck, why be mad?

The pontoon was fairly new. It had a built in radio and CD player. Billy cranked up the music and started out toward the island. Skyler and Billy seemed pretty cozy. She was sitting in his lap while he drove. Allie had begun to loosen up and was at the front of the boat dancing along to the radio.

It didn't take long to get to Fox Bend. Once they anchored the boat, Skyler and Billy went for a walk leaving Alex and Allie behind.

"Those two are something else." Allie laughed as she watched Skyler and Billy scamper off like two children heading off on a new adventure.

"Well, it gives us some alone time." Alex lounged back on the seat and turned Allie around to lounge back on him. "Let's just lay here, relax, and look up at the stars."

Allie didn't argue, she closed her eyes and enjoyed having Alex hold her. "Don't let me down Alex." Allie whispered. She didn't want to talk about all that she had found out that day. Allie just wanted to let Alex know exactly what she expected of him. She needed to believe in Alex. She had been disappointed so many times before and she needed this to be different.

Alex kissed her neck and whispered back, "Don't ever give up on me, or on us." Now they both knew what the other needed. Allie needed reassurance that Alex would be loyal, and Alex needed to know that Allie would always have his back.

CHAPTER FOURTEEN

As weeks went by it seemed that both couples' relationships were getting stronger. Billy and Skyler spent all their time together when he wasn't working. They were inseparable. Billy was taking more time off, and Skyler often stayed the night with him instead of going home to her condo. Allie and Skyler tried not to think about the threats that Allie had overheard Veronica declaring. Instead, they just enjoyed spending their spare time with the guys. It was the end of July, and this was the weekend they were planning on staying off the resort with Eve. Friday night, after everyone got off work, the four of them were going to jump into Eve's car, and take a mini vacation away from the resort.

Summer at The Point

It was a bright, sunny day and Allie and Skyler had decided to spend it laid out by the lake.

"Tomorrow night should be fun. It's nice of Eve to let us stay with her." Allie flipped over to tan her back.

"I know. I'm excited. Thank goodness tomorrow is Friday." Skyler sat up to rub sunscreen on her legs. "I'm so glad you have today off. You know, I used to stay at Eve's a lot when I was younger. My dad isn't big on me hanging around the employees here, but it was always different with Eve." Skyler started an explanation. "See, my dad and Eve go way back. They were actually lovers in high school. From what I've gotten from my mother, it seems they were pretty tight. My dad was the valedictorian, and Eve was the fearless bad girl. They did not fit together at all, but opposites attract, I guess. Anyway, he trusts her, and I know too much, so he's always been cool with me staying with her."

"Wow. I never would have guessed." Allie responded.

******

Meanwhile, Veronica and Marcy were growing impatient. They sat on the bank and watched Allie and Skyler as they sunbathed and laughed about how wonderful everything had been going. "Ugh, Veronica, how much longer before Alex is mine again. I'm tired of waiting. He's spending too much time with her. John said he can't even get Alex to hang out with him at all. He's says he's always too busy, or he had made plans with Allie." Marcy let down her hair, and ran her fingers through it.

"Patience Marcy. Remember the plan that I mentioned earlier this summer? I am pretty sure it is about to take effect. Want to hear it?" Veronica smirked and Marcy nodded. "I've been planning this all year long. You see, my mom works at the health department and I was able to get some out of date birth control pills. I also swiped my mom's fertility pills out of the cabinet. They were left over from her last attempt to have a baby." It was a little scary to Marcy that Veronica had put this much thought into her plan to hurt Skyler. "Well, I carefully peeled the entire foil off of the back, and replaced the pills with fertility enhancing pills. Then I glued the foil back onto the pack. I was able to do four packs. So, when I got to the resort this summer, I snuck into Skyler's room at the condo, and swapped out her birth control pills for the fake ones. Now when I was developing this plan, Billy wasn't even in the picture, but I knew some dumb fool would be. I got nervous when she was with Braxton for a while, but I knew that wasn't serious." Veronica twirled her hair as she rambled. "You see Marcy, if Skyler gets pregnant her dad will kick her out, and Billy will think she lied to him. He will then be done with her. I can't see this plan failing. Skyler Richardson's perfect life won't be perfect for long." Veronica cackled and imagined Skyler having no place to turn.

"That's genius, but it still doesn't solve my problem.

Summer at The Point

What about Alex?" Marcy was once again whining.

"Marcy, get a grip. John is going to meet Alex tomorrow after he gets off, and take him out to The Point with the old gang. Alex can't keep saying no, John promised he would get him to hang out this time, no matter what it takes." Veronica loved drama, and drama suited her. "Those two won't be smiling much longer." Veronica pointed towards Allie and Skyler tanning by the water.

Allie and Skyler spent the entire afternoon tanning, before showering. Afterwards, they would meet Billy and Alex for dinner and a movie in Billy's room.

Skyler and Allie took their time getting ready in the dorm. Then, at seven o'clock, they walked out to the courtyard and headed to Billy's room.

"Hey you." Alex came up behind Allie and hugged her tight. "Did I scare you?"

Skyler and Allie were walking to Billy's when Alex had run up behind them. "A little, but I'm over it. I missed you." Allie kissed Alex then held his hand as they continued walking.

"Knock, knock. We're here." Skyler opened Billy's unlocked door. Billy had a pizza sitting on the side table with a DVD on top.

"Hope this works for you guys." Billy held up a comedy. "My roommate moved in with someone else, so I've got the place to myself now." He pointed at the changes he had made to create more space.

"Looks nice." Skyler commented on the décor.

Alex picked up a pillow off the bed and whacked Allie with it. "Ouch, Alex. You're going to pay for that." Allie picked up a pillow and fought back.

The two fought with pillows for a few minutes then followed that with a tickle fight.

"Okay children, let's eat." Billy passed plates around. "So tomorrow night, we are staying at Eve's, right Alex."

"Yeah, she's going to pick us up in front of the restaurant at eleven. Allie's the last to get off, so once she's done, we'll leave." Alex kissed Allie on the cheek. "I'll get everyone's stuff together, and pack the car tomorrow afternoon. Ya'll just meet me in front of the bowling alley at three."

"Okay, that sounds fine. I work from four until ten. Skyler are you meeting me then?" Billy wanted Skyler to come to the restaurant and wait with him after he got off.

"Yeah, I'll be up there at ten, and you and I can wait in the restaurant for everyone else. Alex where will you be?" Skyler asked. She didn't want to take any chances that Alex would go off with John.

"I'm working from four until nine, then I was going to hang out with Braxton for a little while. He's been pretty lonely lately and I told him that I would come by and see him before I left. He knows I'm staying with Eve, but he doesn't know that ya'll are. I'll be there to meet you guys at eleven." Alex felt bad about leaving Braxton out. After all, Braxton was one of the first guys at the resort to befriend him and he knew that he was taking the changes pretty hard.

"Okay, well that's nice of you." Skyler had finished talking about tomorrow. "Push play, Billy."

They watched the movie and when it was over, Allie went back to her room, and Alex followed her. "It's twelve o'clock. Guess I should get some rest. I'll see you at three tomorrow."

"Are you looking forward to staying at Eve's?" Alex wanted to make sure it was what Allie wanted.

"Yes, of course. I think we'll have a good time." Allie could feel the excitement already bubbling inside her. She couldn't wait for tomorrow.

"Allie, can I talk to you for a minute before I leave?" Alex had a few things on his mind.

"Sure. Is something wrong?" Allie could not tell where the conversation was headed.

"We've been hanging out for a month or so and things have been going really well. I guess what I want to say is, I want you to officially be my girlfriend. If you are ready, that is. Its just, everyone thinks we are a couple, but I'm not sure if we are. Am I making any sense?" Alex stepped towards Allie.

"I would love to be your girlfriend, Alex." Allie kissed Alex. "I'll see you tomorrow. Goodnight."

"Goodnight sweetheart." Alex kissed her cheek, and walked back towards Billy's dorm. Since Billy and Skyler had been dating, Alex has been staying there instead of Braxton's cabin.

Alex arrived at Billy's door and he overheard Skyler and Billy talking. He could tell that they wanted to be alone. Even though he wasn't as close with Braxton as he had been in the past, Alex hoped he still had a place to stay. Alex made his way through the courtyard and back down the hill to the Davis cabin.

Alex peeped in through the sliding glass door. Braxton was still up watching television, and Marcy was with him. "Hey man, come on in." Braxton waived for Alex to come in. "What's up man? Wasn't expecting to see you tonight."

"I missed my ride with Eve. She thought I was staying here." Alex didn't want to tell Braxton that he was planning on staying with Billy, but since Skyler was sleeping over, his plans had changed.

"Hey Alex. It's good to see you." Marcy stated. "Have you seen John? You know he's back." Marcy moved away from Braxton, and focused all of her attention on

Summer at The Point

Alex.

"I've run across him a few times." Alex didn't want to be around Marcy, and he knew Braxton really didn't either. "Look man, if your busy here I can go stay somewhere else." Marcy was always just the fall back girl when the guys first choice was unavailable.

"She was just leaving dude. You can crash here." Braxton signaled for Marcy to get lost. "You know how it is Marcy. Bros come first."

Marcy was more aggravated than ever. She was going to find Veronica and John. She wanted to make sure the intervention happened soon. Marcy went to Veronica's to vent about Braxton kicking her out. John was there and so were Katy and Bobby.

"John, I hope you brought the good stuff. I will get my Alex back. And you are all going to help me." Marcy was determined.

******

Alex slept late the next morning before cooking breakfast for himself and Braxton. The two boys talked about nonsense, and killed some time before Alex had to go into work.

The restaurant was busy and the night flew by. Alex wasn't even able to take his normal fifteen-minute break. He was relieved when his shift finally came to an end.

140

Alex hung up his apron and punched the clock. It was nine o'clock and he was going to meet Braxton just like he had planned. To avoid the crowd, he took the back door, and walked the golf cart path toward Braxton's cabin. He had two hours before he had to meet Allie and the gang.

"Hey man, where are you headed?" John pulled up beside Alex on the golf cart. John had long stringy hair that he kept pulled back tight in a low ponytail. He had a cigarette in one hand and a beer in the other. He's jeans were torn and his shirt was a faded black with a band's name written on the back along with tour dates. "Come with me for a little while. I got Veronica, Katy, Bobby, and Marcy waiting for me at The Point."

"I got plans man. Maybe some other time." Alex walked away from John.

"I never thought you, of all people, would let a girl change you. Ditch her man. You need to hang with the old gang tonight." John was doing his best to persuade Alex to come with him.

"It's not just Allie. I am staying at Eve's tonight and I have to meet her at eleven." Alex had no intentions of getting on Eve's bad side. He knew all to well what that was like.

"Jump on, I'll have you back in time. Don't be a wimp man." John always got his way. Alex got on the golf cart and forgot about his loyalty to not only Allie, but

Braxton as well.

They sped haphazardly across the resort.

"Ha ha, look who I picked up." John called attention to his guest.

"Well, look who it is. I'm glad you decided to join us." Veronica ran her pointed finger down Alex's shirt.

"I'm only going to hang for a little bit. I have to be back at the restaurant by eleven or Eve will have my ass." Alex grabbed a beer and sat next to John.

Marcy was eyeballing him from across the rocks. She was already drunk and stumbling over her words. "Hey pretty boy. Come sit with me for a while."

"She's calling you, buddy. Go get her." John gently nudged Alex, but it knocked him down nonetheless. Alex walked over, and took a seat next to his ex-girlfriend. He knew it was wrong, but at that moment, it felt right. It was as if he fell right back into the lifestyle he was living last summer.

Time flew by, and as Alex had a couple of beers, he began to loosen up. Marcy continued to flirt with him, she teased and taunted him like she used to. Then, Alex kissed Marcy, not because he cared for her, but because it was what he knew. That's who he was. He thought he was beginning to better himself, but he kept going back time after time.

"This is how it's supposed to be man." John declared as he brought Alex another drink. "You're one of us."

Alex stood up and walked over to John to bum a cigarette. He patted him on the back and said, "I missed you man."

"I know, seriously. The summer is almost over. It's about time we hung out." John took a hit off his cigarette. "It's almost eleven dude, what are you going to do?"

"About what? Let's go swimming man." Alex jumped in head first without giving it a second thought.

******

Just on the other side of the resort at the restaurant, Eve had pulled into the parking lot. Skyler and Billy were sitting on the curb outside the main entrance. Inside Allie was getting her purse out of her locker and would soon be ready to leave.

"Where's Alex?" Eve quickly asked Skyler. She wanted to know if there were any concerns before Allie was outside.

"We haven't seen him. He said he was going to meet Braxton, and that he would be back here by eleven." Skyler hoped he followed through with his plans.

"Isn't that Braxton inside with his dad?" Eve pointed out. She could see him through the glass window. He was sitting at a table with Mr. Davis, and there was no sign of Alex.

"Oh no, I was afraid of this. Skyler, I'm going to borrow your golf cart for awhile." Billy had a pretty good idea about where Alex was, and what he was doing. "I'll be back."

As Billy was pulling out of the parking lot, Allie walked out of the door. "Where's Billy going?"

"He is just going to get something he left in his room." Skyler responded after a little hesitation.

"Hey Miss Allie. How are you?" Eve changed the subject.

"I'm okay. Where's Alex?" Allie looked around, and when she didn't see him, a sinking feeling took control of her stomach once again. Even though she didn't know where he was, for some reason she felt hurt and betrayed like she used to feel with Eric.

"He'll be here soon. How was work?" Skyler was trying to take the focus off Alex's absence.

"Look, Billy's coming back." Allie called out. Skyler worried that he had returned so quickly and that he was alone.

Billy didn't speak to Skyler or Allie. Instead he asked Eve to come with him. Billy had found Alex, and he hoped Eve could talk some sense into him. Once on the golf cart Billy explained to Eve what it was that he saw. Alex was with Marcy and John at The Point.

Billy and Eve arrived at The Point. "Alex Owen Shea! Get your underage, skinny ass out of the water and over here now." Eve was incredibly angry. "And the rest of you need to get the hell away from him right now." Alex had been smoking, drinking, and acting like a fool in front of a crowd of members' children. Eve recognized every single face, and threatened to alert parents if Alex didn't come with her. "How stupid can you be?" Eve continued to lecture Alex as she attempted to pull him toward the golf cart. He was soaking wet and extremely pissed.

"I'm staying here." Alex argued back with slurred speech. "You can't tell me what to do." Eve was amazed at how easily John could manipulate Alex. "I'm with my friends."

"Friends. These people are not your friends, Alex." Billy chimed in. "Allie and Skyler are waiting for you. They are your friends. Let's go man." Billy attempted to encourage Alex to come with them. He walked toward him, and placed a hand on Alex's back to guide him to the golf cart.

"Get off of me man." Alex stumbled and fell to the ground.

"It's getting late and I don't have time for this, Alex." Eve argued.

Summer at The Point

"Hey lady, he said he wasn't going." John called out.

"Do you have any idea how easy it would be for me to get your ass kicked off the resort a second time?" Eve threatened. "I suggest the rest of you get out of here."

"We'll just find another place to party." John threw a beer can at Eve before gathering his friends and heading away from The Point.

Once Alex vomited and composed himself somewhat, Billy and Eve were able to direct him onto the golf cart. Once he was situated, they rode back up to the restaurant. Alex did not say a word to anyone. He made no attempt to explain himself.

Billy parked the golf cart next to Eve's car. Alex attempted to stand. He came face to face with Skyler and Allie. It was obvious he was ashamed of something as he quickly turned away. Allie wasn't stupid, she knew that something was apparently wrong since he was adamant about distancing himself from her.

"Where have you been? You look and smell terrible, and you're wet!" Skyler commented about Alex's disheveled appearance.

Alex just closed his eyes and shook his head. He was a little dizzy, so he decided to take a seat on the curb. "I don't think I'm going to go with you guys." Alex laid back and sat his hat on his face.

"You're definitely coming with us, young man. I've had
146

enough of your crap." Eve was still angry, and Alex would stay at that resort over her dead body. "You and Allie need to talk." Eve looked around and noticed that Allie had walked off at some point during the conversation. "Allie!" Eve called out.

It was too late. Allie didn't need to hear what Alex or anyone else had to say. She knew in her gut that he had done something wrong. Allie was mad at herself for trusting that Alex wouldn't let her down, when in fact he did just that. She didn't need to know how bad he screwed up. She was hurt and nothing would change that. Allie was walking back to her room. Alex was dead to her at this moment. "It figures." She thought out loud. "As soon as I open up, I get hurt." Allie was getting a little too used to people betraying her trust. She knew that Alex was younger, and she was warned that he could be easily swayed; but she didn't listen. Allie hoped that DJ was out; she wanted the room to herself for the night. She didn't feel like filling anyone in on what happened.

Back at the car, Eve and Billy searched around the restaurant while Skyler spoke her mind to Alex. "Do you know how hard it was for her to open up to you and really trust you? You don't pretend to want to be with someone, and then stab them in the back as soon as you get the chance. She would never have hurt you like that. Damn Alex. What were you thinking?" Skyler could not believe that Alex would do something so incredibly stupid.

"I don't need to hear this from you Skyler. I know I messed up." Alex vomited once more. "I just want to be alone. Eve, can you take me home?" Alex was frustrated at himself. He knew he screwed up, but he didn't want a lecture.

"You are staying with me, and so are Skyler and Billy. I guess Allie won't be staying now. We do need to find her, and make sure she's okay before we leave." Eve looked at Alex and signaled him to get into the car. "I'm sure she went back to her room. We can check there first."

Alex and Skyler got in Eve's car and drove to the employee cabins. Billy drove the golf cart so he could drop it off behind Skyler's condo.

"I'll go talk to her." Skyler volunteered. Alex was sitting in the backseat with his head dropped between his knees. "Is that okay with you Alex?"

"I don't care. Do what you want." Alex was starting to take his frustration out on everyone. "I just want to go to bed."

"Don't you want to talk to her too?" Skyler asked Alex.

"I think he needs to get himself together first." Eve suggested. "You go talk to her Skyler and convince her to come stay with us."

"Wait!" Alex said a little louder than necessary, which startled Skyler.

148

"Yeah?" Skyler said annoyed with Alex.

"Tell her I'm sorry." Alex pleaded.

"I'll tell her you know you were wrong, but I refuse to do your dirty work. Okay, I'll be right back." Skyler jogged away from the car, and to the side entrance of the living quarters.

CHAPTER FIFTEEN

"Hey girl. Are you in there?" Skyler was banging on Allie's door so loud the neighbor's came to see what the commotion was all about.

The door cracked open slightly, and Skyler slipped into Allie's dark dorm room. Skyler didn't need light to see that Allie was upset and had obviously been crying. "Allie, are you okay? You ran off so fast." Skyler asked.

Allie didn't want to talk about it. She was mad at herself for letting her guard down too soon. "I'm fine. He had a right to hang out with his old friends. I can't fault him for that." Allie was trying to keep busy while avoiding eye contact with Skyler.

"Right. But, he should not have acted the way he did. Drinking and doing, goodness knows, what else. He's not used to having someone like you in his life. He needs to appreciate you and the time you guys have been spending together." Skyler stepped in front of Allie to force her to look up at her. "He knows he screwed up. I'm pretty sure some shady things went down, but I don't know the details. If I find out everything that happened, do you want to know? Are you planning on talking to him?"

"I honestly don't know Skyler. I mean, I want to be understanding and forgiving, but I've been hurt so many times before. And, I have a gut feeling the something happened between him and Marcy. That's just not cool. I'm not going to be with a guy like that. I don't like playing games." Allie picked up some dirty clothes off the floor and threw them into the hamper. "I hope you guys have fun with Eve tonight." Allie continued to fumble around clothes, trying to stay busy. "And yeah, I guess I do want to know everything. It's better to hear it all from you rather than getting it through campground rumors."

"You are more than welcome to come stay. Eve wants you to, and Billy and I do too. I'm sure Alex does as well. In my personal opinion, I think Alex really cares about you and it scares him. I think what he was pulled into tonight was safe and familiar to him. With you it is different, it's real." Skyler knew that Allie and Alex loved each other. You could see the sparks between them

Summer at The Point

and everyone knew it was real. "Guys just do stupid things sometimes. You should come to Eve's and talk to him."

Allie stopped cleaning and sighed. "I do want to talk to him. He once asked me not to give up on him, and I promised that I wouldn't. I care more for Alex than I ever cared for Eric. I just wish he wasn't so easily manipulated by these upper-class, white-trash folks." Allie smirked at Skyler, she didn't even know if what she had said made any since at all.

"Upper-class trash, huh? That's an interesting description." Skyler laughed to lighten the mood. "Come with us girl, and get your answers." Skyler grabbed Allie's duffel bag off the floor and packed some basic necessities.

Allie didn't argue. She helped gather her things and followed Skyler out the door. "I hope I don't regret this." Allie mumbled as she saw Alex leaning up against Eve's car smoking a cigarette. His eyes were blood-shot and his clothes were still damp, dirty and wrinkled. A sinking sick feeling returned to her stomach when she thought about Alex being with Marcy tonight. She couldn't focus her thoughts, or generate any words that could help fix things between them. Allie climbed into the backseat beside Skyler without any acknowledgement of Alex. Billy got in on the other side of Skyler leaving the front seat open for Alex.

Everyone got into the car. A night off the resort was

definitely something Allie had looked forward to. She just wished the circumstances were different. The car ride was filled with awkward silence, and the only sound being the soft rock music on the radio. Alex kept his head on the window, dozing off and then awakening from his head bumping the glass every time Eve hit a dip in the road. Billy and Skyler were holding hands, enjoying being together. Eve kept trying to start a conversation, but no one was interested in talking. Allie alternated starring out the window with starring at Alex. The short drive to Eve's house seemed like an eternity.

Once they finally arrived, the backseat emptied and Eve went to open the front door. However, Alex got out of the car only to take a seat on the bench under an old oak tree. "I'll be inside in a minute." Allie whispered to Skyler. Skyler nodded in understanding.

"Mind if I sit." Allie signaled toward the bench.

Alex shrugged. "You'll probably change your mind in a minute." He patted the bench letting her know that he did want her to sit next to him. Alex was more alert now, and was better able to talk about what had happened.

"I'm ready to listen. I want you to be honest with me." Allie tried to keep her voice steady as she continued to fight back the tears that had been trying to come out all night.

"I kissed her." That was all Alex needed to say. Allie didn't think she could listen to anymore. She was glad she was sitting otherwise her knees surely would have buckled. She wanted him to be honest, but she underestimated her readiness to hear what he had to say. "It didn't mean anything. I was in the mindset of last summer. I was with my old gang, and I gave into temptations. I want you to know that I didn't mean for it to happen. I don't know how I let it happen."

"But it did happen Alex. You convinced me that I could trust you, and that you would never hurt me like Eric had. I opened up to you. Maybe that was a mistake. Maybe I had you all wrong. I thought you cared for me like I care for you." Allie wanted to fix things, but she also wanted Alex to man-up, and know that she deserved to be treated better. If this were any other guy, Allie wouldn't put up with it; at least that is what she was telling herself.

"I do care. I have been wanting to tell you something, but I've been afraid. I went back to the familiar instead of having faith in something new. I was wrong." Alex stood up and then grabbed Allie's hands and pulled her up. They faced each other, and Alex swept her hair away from her face. "The other night, when I asked you to be my girlfriend, there was something else that I was really wanting to say." Alex took a deep breath. "I love you. I've never told a girl that before. It scares the hell out of me."

"Really? You have a funny way of showing it." Allie

replied sarcastically. "You know, you did ask me never to give up on you. So for that I will give you another chance. By the way Alex. I love you too." As Allie spoke those words the tears that she had been holding back finally surfaced. She was feeling an array of emotions; she was angry, jealous, happy, and in love all at once. Alex kissed Allie, and it seemed that for that moment all was right in their world despite how wrong it really was. They were away from the drama for now, so this moment was theirs, and no one could steal that away from them.

Allie pulled away once her heart was no longer racing.

"Things at the resort are going to be tough." Allie warned Alex. "Marcy will expect you to be back with her. I don't want any trouble with anyone. The summer is nearly over."

"Don't worry about all of that. I'll take care of it. I am more concerned with what is going to happen with us when the summer is over. I'll still be here while you go back to college." Allie was starting to get a better idea of what was worrying Alex.

"I'll come home as often as I can, and you can visit me. It can work. Let's just live day to day and enjoy being with each other." Allie hugged her love. "We should continue talking about this tomorrow, I think we've covered enough tonight." Allie steered Alex toward the door, and they walked into Eve's house with wet faces from tears, and smiles that assured everyone that this love was for real.

Of course, it still bothered Allie that Alex had kissed Marcy. Sure, there were things from that night that she did not know about, but Allie did not need to know. She loved Alex so much that the thought of being without him caused a pain in her chest and a sinking feeling in her stomach. It is amazing how strong one person can feel about another. Now that Allie was letting herself feel, she knew what it was like to love someone with every fiber of your being. It did not matter to her that he was younger. She did not care that people talked down on the way they looked together. All that mattered was the love that they felt for each other. Allie was not naïve. She understood that Alex was young and could easily stray away and end up hurting her again, but the benefits far out way the consequence.

"Breakfast anyone." Eve had a frying pan in one hand and a carton of eggs in the other.

"It's two a.m." Skyler pointed out.

"Breakfast is good at any time. Come on. Alex, you fry the bacon. I'll scramble the eggs. Billy, put some bread in the toaster. Girls, straighten up the table." Eve was throwing out commands like a pro and everyone had seemed to put the night's drama behind them for now.

While Allie and Skyler were cleaning the kitchen table, Skyler motioned for Allie to come into the living room so she could talk with her about something.

"Is something wrong Skyler?" Allie could see that something was bothering her and doubted that it had anything to do with herself or Alex.

"I know you have a lot going on right now, but I'm freaking out a little." Skyler hands were a little shaky and she obviously needed to get something off her chest.

"What is it?" Allie asked.

"I'm late. Very late." Skyler was shaking the entire time she was telling this to Allie. "And I'm nauseated and scared." Skyler led Allie to the back of the house and into Alex's room. "You don't think? I mean, I can't be. I'm on the... well you know. What should I do?" Skyler was rambling.

Allie grabbed Skyler's wrists. "Calm down." She whispered in a firm voice. "Wait here." Allie let go of Skyler and went back into the kitchen. She loved the smell of breakfast food. It was homey and comforting. "Eve, is there a convenience store around here that would be open now?"

Eve turned away from the eggs to address Allie. "Yeah, there is one about six miles out heading toward the interstate. It's open twenty-four hours." Eve responded puzzled as to what Allie might need at such a late hour. "Allie what could be so important that you need to get

it right now?"

Allie had to think of something quick. "Chocolate milk. I just can't eat breakfast without it. A little odd, huh?" Allie was thinking how incredibly cheesy she sounded, but she hadn't had much time to prepare a rouse to get out of the house.

"Here are the keys." Eve tossed the keys at Allie. "Can you grab me some cigarettes and a roll of toilet paper while you're out? Food should be ready when you get back. Skyler, are you riding with her?"

"Yeah, Allie I'll ride with you." Skyler hesitated for a moment trying to take in what had just happened. Then she grabbed her purse and her phone before following Allie out the front door.

"Thanks Eve. We'll be right back." Allie called out as they left, she was a little frantic but appeared in control as she headed off to the store.

Allie started the car, and pulled slowly up the hill and out of the driveway. Driving someone else's car always made her nervous. "So, I take it we aren't going for chocolate milk?" Skyler asked.

"Well, we will have to get some now, but you should know what we are really going to get. I had to think of something quick, and that was the first thing that came to mind." Allie was nervous, excited, and a little panicky. "First answer this. You are on the pill, right?"

Skyler began to dig through her purse for the evidence. "Yeah, see." Skyler handed her current pack to Allie.

There were no other cars on the road and Allie hoped that no cops were around either. She sped around the curves, and down the country roads. Allie was nervous for Skyler and wished that Skyler had come to her sooner.

Allie felt the pack in her hand. "I'll look at it when we get there. Maybe the pack is expired. Or maybe, we are just freaking out for no reason. How long have you been feeling like this. How late are you?" Allie was trying to think rationally.

"I wanted to talk to you about it sooner, I had prepared to talk to you about it tonight. But then everything happened with Alex, and I didn't want to burden you with my issues too. I'm just over three weeks late. I had stopped taking my pills at this spring because I felt like they were causing me to gain weight. Then I started them again at the start of summer. I thought they were pretty effective."

"I'm sorry. Tonight did get a little out of hand." Allie apologized for not being able to talk with her friend sooner.

"It's not your fault." Skyler reassured her.

"Well maybe since you were off the pill for a while, your cycle is just off. You'll probably start soon. Anyway we are about to get our answer as soon as we find the store. Here we go." Allie noticed some lights just over the hill. "That must be it, up here on the left. Looks sort of rundown, I hope they have what we need."

They arrived at Mr. Pete's 24/7 Country Mart and the two quickly ran inside. They walked around the store and Allie quickly noticed that what they came for was behind the counter. She squinted to see the choices, then she looked at Skyler and shrugged. "Which one?" Allie asked.

"One of each. I want to be sure." Skyler was serious.

Allie decided to wait on the milk and cigarettes until after they had handled business. "I need to get a pregnancy test. One of each brand please." They were nearly ten dollars apiece after tax, and Skyler handed the clerk two twenties and a ten. "Do you have a bathroom?" The clerk pointed toward the back of the store.

Allie grabbed Skyler's arm and the bag of tests. They went into the family bathroom and locked the door. Skyler completed all three of the tests and then they were forced to sit impatiently waiting for the results. Both of them were leaned over the samples to see the image that might appear. One by one, each stick revealed Skyler's fate.

"There's your answer." Allie stated. "How did it happen? Not how but...wow! I don't know what to say." Allie was at a loss for words when each test showed that Skyler was definitely pregnant.

"I can't believe this." Skyler took a seat on the sink.

"What did I do with your pills?" Allie felt her pockets and looked in her purse. "Here they are." Allie examined the pack to see if they had perhaps expired. "No. They are still in date. Ouch!" Allie cried out. "The foil cut me." She fiddled with the part that sliced her finger and she was able to pull the entire back of the package off. "Is it supposed to do that?" Allie handed the two parts to Skyler. "It looks like the back was taken off and glued back on. That's odd, it's almost like someone has tampered with it."

"I got these as samples from the doctor's office. You know the last pack I had was the same way. Almost like a package defect." Skyler recalled.

"You might need to let your MD know about it. The whole lot might have been fooled with." Allie suggested. "What do you need me to do?"

"I have no idea." Skyler replied still in shock from the results.

"Are you going to tell your parents? What about Billy?" Allie asked with concern.

"I don't know yet. I need to think first. I'll probably let Billy know tonight. I'm scared Allie. I hadn't planned for a baby. There is no way I can handle this right now."

Skyler was disappointed in herself for letting something like this happen. Her whole life was about to change, and not in the ways she had planned. They trashed the boxes, but Skyler decided to keep the evidence in a paper bag.

"I'm here for you. That's what friends are for." Allie assured her friend. " Do you want to sit here for a bit, or are you ready to go on back?" Allie offered Skyler a hug. "I'll sit as long as you need me to."

"It's okay. We can go on back." Skyler took a deep breath. Then she wet a paper towel and wiped her face. "I'll go wait in the car while you get the stuff if that's okay. I feel even more nauseated now."

"Okay." As Skyler walked to the car, Allie grabbed the chocolate milk, Eve's cigarettes and toilet paper. The car ride back to Eve's was quiet. Neither girl knew what to say at this time. Skyler was planning on breaking free from her parents and going out on her own, but she wondered if that was still an option. Could she afford to take care of herself and a baby? Would her parents force her to leave now that she has shamed them? What about Billy? Would he expect her to marry him? So much was left to question. Skyler hoped she had the strength to accomplish what had to be done. "We're back." Allie announced to Skyler as they pulled into the driveway. The ride back seemed much shorter this time. Skyler was anxious about going inside and having to figure out the best time to tell Billy.

"Just in time." Eve stated as the girls walked in. They all sat down at the table to enjoy a nice hot breakfast. Eve sat at the head of the table and smiled up at the four young adults eating alongside of her. Eve noticed something was troubling Skyler. She gave her a concerning look, but decided to wait until tomorrow before any more drama was addressed. Eve blessed the food and everyone began their meal.

Summer at The Point

CHAPTER SIXTEEN

While Skyler and Allie were snuggled next to there lovers at Eve's, the member girls were still partying hard at the resort. After leaving The Point they regrouped by the golf cart rack. Marcy was angered that Alex was pulled away from her once again. She was tired of having to compete for him. As far as she was concerned Alex was hers, and she was not willing to share. "I'm going to figure out a way to really burn Allie, and get her away from Alex for good." Marcy promised John, Veronica, and any other person willing to listen. Her eyes were heavy and her speech slow and slurred. "I think it's ridiculous that she is chasing after someone so much younger than her. Kind of gross, if you ask me." Marcy was the type who rambled and talked excessively when inebriated. "Yep, I'm going to get her good. She's going to be sorry she messed with my guy."

"Forget about it Marcy. The summer is almost over." Veronica interrupted. "She'll be gone then and he won't have a choice but to come back to you." Veronica was tired of hearing Marcy whine. She figured pointing out the obvious and straying away from evil plans would put Marcy's focus back on Veronica's concerns. "I wonder how things are going with Skyler and Billy."

"I'm going back to the cabin. I'm over it. All you care about is yourself. You never had any intention of helping me get Alex back." Marcy got up and climbed into her golf cart. "If I have to back off Allie and Alex, then you should quit scheming too." Marcy sped off leaving the rest of the gang behind. She had enough for the night and she wanted to be alone and think of a way to get Alex back, other than just waiting it out.

"Whatever Marcy. We'll be best friends again in the morning." Veronica called out as Marcy drove away. "She needs to sleep it off. She always gets a little nutty when she's been up this long." Veronica explained to the gang. "Anyway, I think I'm going to head back too. I'll catch up with you guys tomorrow." Veronica was annoyed at the way Marcy acted. She didn't feel like hanging out anymore. Instead, she wanted to rest up for tomorrow. Veronica left the golf cart behind and decided to walk back up to the cabin. She noticed Skyler's parents were still awake, so she decided to eavesdrop on their conversation. Veronica snuck up the back steps and took a seat next to the door of the screened-in porch.

"It's your fault she's like this Patty, running off with those slackers. She needs to begin focusing on her future. I try to set boundaries, then you undermine me and let her do whatever she wants." Skyler's dad was frustrated that Skyler never came home. He felt that Skyler's mom was inconsistent with curfews and boundaries. "When I was her age I was striving to grow, change, and make my dreams and my father's dreams come true. She is acting out and embarrassing our family, and I will not put up with it any longer." He slammed the bedroom door and left Mrs. Richardson sobbing in the kitchen.

Veronica snuck off without being noticed. She smirked as she thought about her plan. "Wait until she gets pregnant. Ha! Then he really will freak out." Veronica said out loud to herself. "And Billy and Braxton will be up for grabs." Veronica smiled as she felt her scheme was flawless.

On her way back across the campground Veronica overheard a noise in the bushes. It sounded as if someone was following her. Veronica usually wasn't afraid of anything, but it was late, she was alone, and she feared the worst. "Who's there?" Veronica called out as she sped up her pace.

"Whoa, slow down girl." Braxton Davis made himself visible as he jumped over some fallen branches. "I've been trying to catch you since you left Skyler's. What were you doing there anyway? Hope you weren't causing any trouble."

"Me. Trouble? Of course not. What's it to you anyway? I thought Skyler burned you when she chose Billy." Veronica knew how to hit you where it really stung.

"Ouch girl." Braxton replied. "She may technically be with Billy, but that doesn't mean we don't still have our fun. What Skyler and I have, will never go away, no matter what relationships we're in." Braxton smirked at the thought of his affair with Skyler.

"Kind of like Marcy and Alex, huh?" Veronica suggested.

"Nothing like that. Marcy holds on to the crazy idea of what she used to have with Alex, but Alex and Allie... now that is the real deal. Haven't you seen the way those two look at each other. That is love baby. Marcy doesn't stand a chance." Braxton did know one thing, he was an expert on feelings, and he picked up quickly on emotional vibes. "So why don't you tell me the real reason you were snooping around Skyler's place?"

"Like I would really tell you. You just finished telling me how close you still are with her." Veronica was trying to think of something to justify her being there. "I was just out for a walk and heard voices. The only thing I'm guilty of is eavesdropping. It has nothing to do with Skyler." Veronica hoped this would be enough to throw Braxton off her trail.

"I guess you are innocent this time. Skyler is off the resort anyway." Braxton began to walk alongside Veronica. "Can't wait until she gets back. We haven't had a chance to hang out in the past two weeks. She's been with Billy so much. Plus she's been a little sick lately."

"Sick. What do you mean?" Veronica inquired as if she was concerned.

"Nauseated, dizzy, run-down. Must be some sort of virus." Braxton responded.

"Yeah, probably." Veronica could hardly contain her excitement. This was it. Her plan had worked. But something didn't feel right. Veronica was no longer certain her plan was flawless. "Guess I should get back to the cabin. I'll see you around Braxton." She switched directions and headed home.

"Is something wrong?" Braxton questioned as she walked away.

"She really does have it all, I guess." For once Veronica realized that jealousy had been the factor in all of her scheming. She didn't hate Skyler, she was jealous of everything that she had. Veronica was starting to have a revelation, and perhaps a change of heart. "There is something wrong Braxton, but you need to keep it on the low if I tell you."

"What is it Veronica?" Braxton was becoming a bit irritated.

"Skyler is pregnant Braxton. I'm not even sure she knows yet." Veronica considered this the white flag. She knew that Braxton would always love Skyler no matter what and she figured the same was true for Billy. Skyler was a good person. That was why everyone gravitated towards her. It wasn't her money or looks, it was who she was, and what she was about. Veronica realized that Skyler was a good person. All of a sudden Veronica thought, "What have I done?"

"What are you talking about? All of what? Pregnant? How do you know?" Braxton grabbed hold of Veronica's shoulders. "Start talking woman!"

"I switched out Skyler's birth control with fertility pills. It's been about two months, and I think that is why she is nauseated and sick. Did you and she..." Veronica hoped he would say no.

"Yeah, but it's been a while. It was right after her boating trip with Billy. You don't think?" Braxton responded.

"I don't know. I'm really sorry Braxton. I thought that if Skyler got pregnant, then none of the guys would want anything to do with her. I was jealous. I didn't think." Veronica's mouth poured out her confessions like a draft tap. The alcohol was probably the only reason she was breaking down and letting Braxton in on the secrets she had been keeping.

"You know that I have to tell Skyler right?" Braxton

Summer at The Point

didn't know how he would tell her, but he knew Skyler needed to know.

"Of course." Veronica had no other response. She hadn't cried in years, but she started to feel as if she could. Apparently alcohol helped her get in touch with her emotions.

"Well, maybe I'll keep it under wraps for a while. At least until we find out if she really is pregnant." Braxton put his arm around Veronica's shoulders. "Maybe this is the beginning of a new Veronica?" Braxton suggested hopefully.

"Not hardly. Once I sober up, I'll regret it all I'm sure. Then I'll be the same villain that everyone loves to hate." Veronica rolled her eyes.

"No one hates you Veronica. Is that why you did this? Is that what you think?" Braxton asked, trying to find out a little more about Veronica.

"It doesn't matter. Can you walk me to the cabin? I'm starting to feel a little nauseated myself." Veronica held tight to Braxton as they walked back toward her cabin. At this point Veronica didn't care what Braxton did or didn't tell Skyler. She just wanted to sleep. Once at this cabin Braxton walked Veronica to the door and turned to leave once he knew she would be okay. "Do you think we will ever have our chance, you and me?" Veronica asked Braxton as he walked up the drive.

"Maybe someday Veronica. Who knows?" He shrugged his shoulders, and headed back to the Davis' cabin to call it a night. Braxton knew from experience how new feelings can surface when you least expect them.

******

Allie loved Eve's house. She felt cozy and safe as she laid in bed. She and Alex were in the back bedroom, which was painted a bright blue and accented with white décor.

"Crap!" Allie heard someone remark outside the bedroom. She slipped out of Alex's arms and cracked open the door.

"Skyler, is that you?" Allie whispered. Sound of vomit hitting the toilet was the only noise Allie heard in response to her question. "Are you okay?"

"Guess, it's just morning sickness." Skyler replied as she opened the bathroom door. "I have a confession Allie."

"What is it?" Allie was concerned. "You can tell me."

"I haven't exactly been loyal to Billy. Braxton and I have been seeing each other on the side." Skyler confessed.

"Wow. Skyler that is a lot to swallow." That was all Allie could manage to get out. She took a seat on the side of the bathtub and Skyler took a seat in front of the toilet. Billy didn't deserve this, and she hoped he would never find out.

"Billy has goals, he could help me convince father that I have something to offer the world. He would help me get my voice out there and be heard." Skyler shook her head and took a deep breath. "But still I crave the unconventional fling that I had with Braxton. I know it's dumb. I never thought it would be an issue, but of course now it is. So I have to wonder if it's Billy's or Braxton's." Skyler had tears welling up behind her brown eyes. She obviously had not been to sleep and she looked sick with worry.

"We will figure it out. You need to get some rest Skyler. Tomorrow is a new day." Allie tried to comfort Skyler and convince her to go back to bed. Once that was accomplished, she sighed and wondered how they would fix the situation. For now, she would sleep on it and hope Skyler would do the same. Allie crawled in bed next to Alex and kissed his lips as he lay there sleeping.

CHAPTER SEVENTEEN

The next morning Allie was the last to awaken. She walked into the living room and noticed that Skyler was in the shower, and the boys were already dressed. "Why didn't you wake me?" She asked Alex as she stretched out her arms and took a deep breath.

"You looked so cute and I knew you didn't sleep well. I was getting ready to get you up. Coffee?" He handed her his mug and went to fix himself another cup.

"Thanks." Allie replied as she watched him walk into the kitchen. She hadn't noticed until now how his ankles pop when he walks. Allie giggled and thought to herself how much she really loved Alex. She was beginning to care more for him than she did for herself. It was a love that she has never experienced, and she knew that, even though he screwed up, everything was going to be just fine. She followed him into the kitchen to grab a minute alone with him. "You're great. You know?"

"Hah." Alex chuckled. "Not me. I've been known to make some pretty big mistakes. That is definitely not something a 'GREAT' person would do." Alex shrugged his shoulders. "Do you have a fever? Did you forget about last night?" Alex joked as he placed his hand on her head as if he was checking her temperature.

"I don't care anymore that you messed up. I don't want to know details. I just want to be with you every chance I get. I just want to love you." Allie didn't care that she was putting more effort into the relationship than Alex. All that mattered was that the two of them were together and everything would soon feel right again. Allie grabbed hold of Alex and squeezed him tight. Then she kissed him on the cheek and quickly pulled away as Eve came around the corner to refill her coffee mug.

"Well good morning." Eve smiled at the sight of the happy couple. "Glad to see everyone has moved past last night's festivities."

"Yeah. I got him and that's all that matters." Allie grinned as she held tight to Alex once again.

"I love you Allie. I'm glad we are moving past my screw up. It's pretty cool that you are in such a good mood this morning. I could get used to this." Alex wrapped his arm around Allie's shoulders, leaned in, and kissed the top of her head.

"Just don't get used to needing second chances." Allie said jokingly. She heard the bathroom door open and she knew Skyler was out of the shower. "Guess I need to grab a shower. Anything planned for today?"

"We'll probably go into town and piddle around a little bit before coming back here for a movie night. Then tomorrow, it's us and the coffee shop bright and early."

"I'm definitely not looking forward to tomorrow, but, the rest of it sounds cool. I'll be ready in like thirty minutes." Allie didn't want to hold up the rest of the group. She spent two semesters in a dorm sharing the facilities with about twenty-five other girls, so she knew how to get ready quickly. Allie went into Alex's bedroom to grab a change of clothes and her make-up bag. "Skyler do you have a hair dryer?" Allie called to the bedroom door where Skyler was changing.

"Yeah. I'll leave it on Alex's bed when I'm finished." Skyler replied back.

Allie showered and dressed quickly. She wanted to look good for Alex, and she wanted him to know that it doesn't take her long to look good. In the shower Allie began to think about Skyler's situation that she learned

Summer at The Point

of last night. They would have to talk about that today. Skyler would have to talk about it with someone who could provide a solution, or at least some comforting words. Allie thought that Eve might be a good person to open up to. She wondered what Skyler would think about that.

Allie quickly got out of the shower, dried off, and dressed. Once she was ready, she went into the living room to find Skyler. "Skyler, I need your opinion on something. Can you come with me for a second?" Allie asked. Skyler got up from the couch and followed Allie into Alex's room. "I was thinking," Allie said. "Maybe you could talk to Eve about your situation. She could probably offer you some pretty good advice."

"I've thought about talking to her, but I'm not sure if I'm ready." Skyler replied.

"Well, just go with your gut. I'm here for you." Allie answered back.

The girls returned to the living room. Skyler had an uneasy feeling in her stomach, but she painted on a fake smile for Billy. Eve came into the room holding her purse and car keys. "Okay gang let's go." Eve was ready to get her errands done. "I'm starving, I hope you guys don't mind eating first. Then I have a few things that I want to pick up at the mall."

"I think I could definitely go for some food right about now." Billy remarked.

"I'm still full from last night." Allie whispered to Skyler. "But I'm game."

"Let's do it." Alex grabbed the keys from Eve and they all piled into the car.

The late morning drive to town was nice. The sun was shining bright and everyone was in a pleasant mood. Alex had the radio blaring and the windows rolled down. For the thirty minutes they were in the car, their lives were worry free.

The restaurant they chose was pretty crowded, even for a weekend. But Murphy's was the best restaurant in the area and it was definitely worth waiting for. Alex and Billy went in and put their names on the waiting list. Allie and Skyler took a seat on the curb, and Eve walked around the corner to light a cigarette.

"Can you believe the summer is nearly over?" Allie asked Skyler. "I'm going to miss you guys like crazy. Promise that you will come and visit me."

"I know the time has flown by. As long as everything goes well with the baby, I'll be able to come visit. Wow, it feels weird saying that out loud. 'The baby,' my baby. It still hasn't really sunk in." Skyler looked off into the distance. "I just hope that I'm a strong enough person to do this."

Allie put her hand on Skyler's shoulder. "You are going to be a great mother." Allie reassured. The girls didn't realize that Eve had made her way back behind them and was able to catch the tail end of the conversation.

"Who's going to be a mother?" Eve asked in shock.

Skyler was embarrassed and was looking down at her shoes as she replied, "I'm going to be a mother." She didn't want Eve to find out this way.

"WHAT? Oh, my. When?" Eve was caught off guard.

"Nine months." Skyler replied.

"Yikes! Does Billy know? Have you told him?" Eve asked. "How am I always the last to know?"

"You're actually second. Allie is the only one I have told. I haven't had a chance to tell Billy. I just found out last night." Skyler responded. She definitely wasn't ready to let Eve know that it might not be Billy's baby. "Not sure how I'm feeling about it."

"These things happen Skyler. It's nothing to be ashamed of. You should let Billy know." Eve offered her opinion. "I'm more worried about how your parents, especially your father, are going to handle it. I was twenty when I had Mark. I was lucky, my parents were very supportive. That makes all the difference. I just hope yours will be like that as well." Eve knew how the Richardson's were, and she was concerned for Skyler. She didn't know what had changed Mr. Richardson, but he was a totally different man now compared to the way he was when Eve dated him.

"I'm not going to let them know until I'm showing. That's the plan for now anyway. Then I'll hit them all at once with the baby bomb and my rebellion against everything they are pushing me to do." Skyler was making all kinds of plans in her mind. She was running through conversations with different people, and trying to predict their reactions. Skyler was trying to hide her stress by taking deep breathes and smiling through her fears and concerns.

"Twenty minute wait ladies." Alex announced as he busted through the door with Billy following right behind him. "Skyler are you okay?" Alex grew concerned when noticed Skyler's blank stare and teary eyes.

"I'm fine. Everything is fine. Billy, can you walk with me to the car?" This was it, Skyler was going to tell Billy. There was no point in waiting any longer. She had to at least let him know before they returned to the resort, so what better time than the present. "Excuse us for a second guys." Skyler guided Billy across the crowded parking lot.

"Skyler, is something wrong." Billy asked concerned.

"Billy, have you noticed that I've been feeling nauseated a lot lately, and that my energy has been pretty low?" Skyler started the conversation.

"Yeah, I know that you've been pretty sick lately. Are you okay?" Billy had no idea where this conversation was going.

"I'm... I'm pregnant Billy." Skyler confessed her news and felt a huge weight being lifted off her shoulders. She hated having to keep anything from Billy. She just hoped he would be supportive.

"How did you... when did you... but what about.." He could never get out what he was trying to say.

"Apparently the pills that I have been taking have expired. They actually looked like the package had been tampered with. I just found out yesterday. I wanted to tell you as soon as I knew, but I was scared you wouldn't want to have anything to do with me. I love you Billy." Skyler was more nervous than she had imagined.

Billy pulled Skyler close to him, wrapped his arms around her, and held her for about five minutes before he spoke. "Everything happens for a reason, right? I love you too Skyler. It's all going to work out."

"So you're not mad at me?" Skyler asked.

"Of course not Skyler. I'm actually pretty excited. I mean, I have a few more things to think about now. And, my future plans may change somewhat, but I'm happy about it." Billy kissed her forehead.

"What about my parents? They will never understand. I don't know what I'm supposed to do." Skyler and Billy had a lot to discuss. The restaurant parking lot was hardly the place that

Skyler wanted to have this conversation. Skyler kept having to pause to prevent herself from being over-emotional.

"Table's ready!" Alex called out across the parking lot.

Billy looked at Skyler. "That was fast." He said as he walked toward Alex meeting him halfway. "You guys go ahead and eat. I think Skyler and I need to finish this conversation." Billy handed Alex some cash. "Just get us a little something to go. We'll come in when we're finished here."

"Okay dude, no problem." Alex ran back to Allie and Eve. He filled them in on the plan, and the three of them went to be seated.

Billy quickly returned to Skyler to pick up where they left off. "I told them to get us something to go. So where were we? You are worried about your parents?"

Skyler walked towards a bench to the right of the parking lot by the fountain. "It's just that I have been looking for a way to let my parents knows I don't want to go to college, but I don't know if they can handle all the news at once. Now I'm thinking too that singing is no longer an option since I'm pregnant, so maybe college is the best way to go. I'm just confused Billy. I don't know what I should do." Skyler had tears in her eyes, but she hadn't yet begun to cry. "I feel like I'm letting everyone down." Skyler's spoke those words and her tears broke through simultaneously.

Summer at The Point

"You are not letting anyone down. It's like I keep saying, everything happens for a reason. You're parents will be supportive because they love you. They understand that you need to do what's best for you. Your dad may be a little angry at first, but he'll get over it. Worst case scenario, if they aren't understanding, you'll still have me." Billy hadn't been able to really think about his feelings on the matter, or what he was going to do now. He loved Skyler and he needed to feed her whatever she needed to hear. He knew that he would be able to figure something out that would be great for both of them. However, there was something in the back of Billy's mind that made him ask, "Have you thought about what you're going to tell Braxton?"

"Um, I don't think I should tell him. Do you?" Skyler hoped Billy couldn't see that she still cared for Braxton.

"I think he needs to know. I know you still have feelings for him. Maybe not the same way you did before, but I know that he means a lot to you." It hurt Billy to say that out loud. He loved Skyler, but he understood how difficult it could be to get over someone. Billy knew that Skyler and Braxton had a history, and he could never compete with the bond they had.

"He was my best friend for so long. I guess I should tell him. I just hope you know that there is nothing there romantically between Braxton and myself. I love you Billy. I'm ready to leave everyone else behind as long as I have you." Skyler hugged Billy. "I guess the
182

responsible thing to do is to tell my parents first, and hope they understand. Then I'll talk to Braxton."

"Do you think we should get married?" Billy wanted to show Skyler how serious he was about being there for her and the baby.

"I hadn't thought about that." Skyler lied. "I don't think we should just yet. Maybe we should try living together first. The summer is nearly over. We could both get jobs and rent an apartment. Perhaps my parents will be willing to help us out if they see we have thought it through." Skyler actually liked the idea of moving away, working, and starting her own family.

"If you think that's best, I'm up for it. There is a new hotel opening outside of Richmond. That's were I was planning to go once summer ended. I sent in my resume' for the Restaurant Manager position. I didn't want to say anything until I was sure I got the job. I have an interview on Tuesday, and if all goes well, I'll start the first of September. Would you want to go with me?" Billy never thought he would be experiencing so many challenges at this stage in his life, but he was embracing it.

"To the interview?" Skyler asked.

"Yeah, I figure if I get the job then we can go ahead and start looking for apartments. If it all works out then you can tell your parents on Wednesday. They would probably be a lot more understanding if we already have all the answers to their questions." Billy took a deep breath. "You know, making these plans is kind of nice. It's cool to have something to look forward to."

"I know what you mean. The more we talk about it, the more courageous I'm getting. It's exciting to think about being independent, and breaking free from parental control." Skyler stomach growled. "Oh, wow. Guess I'm more hungry than I thought. Let's go eat. We have a couple days to work out the details. I will go with you Tuesday, and I'll wait before letting anyone else know."

But what Skyler hadn't expected was that Braxton already knew what was going on. He could easily let it slip before Skyler had a chance to talk with her parents.

In the mean time, Skyler and Billy enjoyed being away from the resort for the weekend. They would worry about their problems tomorrow.

CHAPTER EIGHTEEN

Veronica stayed in bed Saturday morning with a horrible headache. She tossed and turned, and stayed balled up with her head under the covers. It was nearly nightfall when she finally crawled out of bed and remembered everything that had happened the night before. Skyler would be back on the resort tomorrow afternoon and Veronica was concerned that Braxton would tell Skyler, despite his promise.

"Oh, my goodness Marcy." Veronica screamed into the phone after she realized the seriousness of telling Braxton what she had done. "She's pregnant. It worked!"

"Wow, I'll be right there. I need details." Marcy hung up the phone, and went to meet Veronica at her cabin. She was surprised when she got there and saw someone had arrived before her. Braxton was waiting on the steps. "Is Veronica expecting you?" Marcy asked Braxton as she climbed up the steps.

"Naw. I haven't knocked yet either. Don't know if I should." Braxton didn't know why he was there. He just thought Veronica might need a friend.

Marcy jumped in front of Braxton and pounded on the screen door. "Veronica." She called out as she opened the door impatiently.

"Hey Marcy... and Braxton? Didn't expect to see you." Veronica was glad to see him, even though she didn't know why he was there.

"We need to talk some more Veronica. I have been freaking out all day about everything with Skyler." Braxton paced around the cabin.

"Wait! You told him." Marcy asked Veronica as she grasped Braxton's shoulder and slung him around to face her. "She told you?" She asked Braxton, not giving Veronica a chance to answer. "What were you thinking?"

"I was frustrated with everything. I had too much to drink. I don't know. The point is I screwed up. She's pregnant, and it might not be Billy's baby. I can't think right now. Talk to her Braxton." Veronica sat down on the coffee table.

"It doesn't matter how I found out. I have been with Skyler a few times the past month and I'm worried. We need to find out for sure if she is pregnant. So we can all quit freaking out, and I'll at least be able to talk with her and see what she thinks. I mean, if I'm the father, my whole life is pretty much over. I think I'm going to be sick now." Braxton sat down next to Veronica. He wasn't ready to be a father, but it made him even more nauseated to think that Billy could be.

"It's all my fault Braxton. For real dude, I'm sorry. I didn't think it through." Veronica was apologetic.

"I see you're the sensitive Veronica again today. What happened, happened. I'm not mad at you, I'm mad at myself. I should have left Skyler alone. She's better off with Billy. You know, I think that no matter the outcome, it's time for me to pull away. I think having me out of the picture would be the best for everyone." It hurt Braxton to even imagine a life without Skyler, but he knew she would be better off if he didn't interfere.

"But what if the baby is yours?" Marcy asked. "You're just going to bail?"

"I'm not even going to let her think of me as an option. I'll lie and play it off however I need to. Once word gets out, everyone will know that it's Billy's baby. If she comes to me and says it's a possibility, then I'll just find

Summer at The Point

a way to convince her that it's not possible. Even if it's mine, Billy would be the better father. Billy will take care of Skyler and the baby. But you two have to promise me that you will keep all of this under wraps. When the rumors start circulating, stand up for me, and keep everyone focused on it being Billy's baby." Braxton hoped this would work. Plus the summer was nearly over and he would no longer have to be around the drama.

"You know if your name comes up, you could always say that you were with me?" Veronica suggested.

Braxton smiled at Veronica. Seeing that she had a caring side to her, made her much more attractive now in Braxton's eyes.

"You would go along with that?" Braxton asked.

"Of course. Anything to help you. And maybe you could be my date for the Miss Rock Springs contest?" Veronica suggested as she grinned at Braxton.

"Hmm.. Siding with the enemy. I can't believe I'm considering it." Braxton nudged Veronica in a flirting manner.

"Maybe the enemy wants to switch to the good guy's team for a change." Veronica responded which surprised herself as well as Marcy and Braxton.

"Wow! What am I witnessing here?" Marcy asked. She was glad that Veronica was able to relax and stop scheming for a change. She hoped her friend would find a guy to keep her from being so hateful. Marcy loved Veronica, but sometimes she was a little too intense, and when she's like that, it tends to bring the worst out in Marcy as well.

"The start of something new. The magic of a summer at The Point." Braxton said as he kissed Veronica. "Finding a special someone in the most unexpected of places. That's the best part of summer."

"I finally got what I wanted. Even though I'm not to proud of the way I got it." Veronica responded.

"Maybe you got what you wanted, because for once you realized how wrong you have been. And you realized you needed to change your ways. No more room raiding, no more sabotaging, no more being hateful to people." Braxton offered his opinion. "I'm not trying to offend you." Braxton didn't know how Veronica would react.

"No, it's okay. You're right. Time to grow up and find fun other ways. Thanks guys. I just hope I didn't screw things up for Skyler too badly." Veronica still felt guilty. "And Marcy, are you prepared to back off too. I mean leave Alex alone for good."

"I'll think about it." Marcy considered.

"I think Skyler will be fine. She's a smart girl. It will turn out fine. You just need to quit worrying. What's done is done." Braxton hugged his new crush. "She'll be back tomorrow afternoon, and we'll see how it all turns out."

******

The weekend flew by and before they knew it, it was time to return to work. Allie and Eve left the house for another early morning at the coffee shop. Alex would be bringing Skyler and Billy later on his uncle's truck.

"Some crazy, busy weekend, huh?" Eve started the conversation as they pulled out of the driveway. "With you and Alex, and then Skyler's big news."

"Yeah. It sure was a lot to take in. I think Alex and I will be okay though. I believe in second chances and soul mates. Eve, you know I'm crazy about Alex." Allie smiled as she thought about her feelings for Alex.

"I know. I also know that he really loves you. He's just a boy, and he does stupid things once in a while. You were right not to give up on him. I can see the sparks between you two. It's refreshing to see." Eve patted Allie on the knee.

"As for Skyler, I'm worried for her. But, I think Billy is a great guy. He'll take care of her. I just hope her parents are supportive. From what I've heard, they are pretty harsh. It seems to be all about image to them. That's sad." Allie thought it was horrible that people could be so judgmental and self absorbed. "Billy has a four year degree, and I'm sure he'll be able to find a pretty good job. And Skyler is a smart girl. She'll find a way to contribute."

"I agree, I think they'll be just fine." Eve agreed.

"Yeah." Allie agreed with her own statement once again.

"So Allie, the Miss Rock Springs contest is coming up. Are you going to enter? It's for employees and members." Eve suggested. "I think you'd have a good chance at winning. They give away money just like the talent show. You could use it for college."

"I don't know. Seems more like Skyler's thing. Plus, I'm not big on the whole public humiliation thing." Allie could picture herself stumbling over her words and making a fool of herself.

"Just give it some thought. You just need an evening gown, bathing suit, and talent. Last day to sign up is next Wednesday." Eve didn't tell Allie that she had already signed her up. She would wait until the last sign-up day, and if Allie hadn't agreed then Eve would let her know.

"Maybe, I'll think about it. I don't have an evening gown though." Allie mentioned.

"I can get you one. Mark's daughter is about your size. Her junior prom gown that she wore last spring is in my closet. I think that would be perfect." Eve could tell Allie was interested.

Summer at The Point

"We'll see." Allie said as they arrived at work. The members were awake and heading down the hill to the coffee shop for their morning caffeine.

Eve opened the back door and Allie started the coffee. As Eve tied on her apron and was about to open the door, she realized that the first customer in line was Mr. Richardson. "This should be interesting." Eve said out loud.

"Good morning, come on in." Eve opened the door and welcomed the morning crowd.

"Eve, I'd like to have a word with you." Mr. Richardson signaled Eve to come outside leaving Allie alone to handle the morning rush.

"Is something wrong?" Eve asked Mr. Richardson.

"Have you seen Skyler? I heard she stayed with you off the resort this weekend. She left without my permission Eve." Mr. Richardson had a stern look on his face.

"She stayed with me, that hasn't been a problem in the past. You need to cut her some slack. Skyler is grown, and she is going to make her own decisions." Eve suggested. "She'll be back this afternoon."

"Who is going to be bringing her back?" He asked.

"Alex, my nephew and his friend Billy." Eve responded. "Now if you don't mind, I need to get back to work." Eve walked away. "The more you hold her back, the more she'll want to pull away."

"Don't let this happen again." Mr. Richardson spoke his final words to Eve before heading back out the door. "Remember, employees are replaceable despite what happened in the past."

"I hope you don't think you can threaten me and get away with it. There is so much I could tell your wife that would just destroy your marriage. So I would keep the threats to a minimum if I were you. You'll get yours Mr. Richardson; that's a promise." Eve mumbled under her breath as she walked behind the counter to help the next customer.

Allie and Eve didn't say much else for the remainder of their shift. Allie was able to see first hand how big of a jerk Mr. Richardson could be. She knew that his offensive manner hurt Eve's feelings, and she knew his wrath would be much worse once Skyler was back on the resort. After the crowd died down, Allie made a phone call to Eve's house. She wanted to warn Skyler about her dad so she would be ready to deal with him.

******

It was nearly three in the afternoon before Alex arrived at the resort with Skyler and Billy. They drove down and parked next to the picnic tables where they met Eve and Allie.

"Hey guys." Allie waived as the gang got out of the

Summer at The Point

car. "Skyler, how are you feeling?"

"I'm great. Just nervous about seeing my dad. I think I'm going to go on back to the cabin now ,and try to talk to him." Skyler replied.

"You going to tell him?" Eve asked.

"No, I'm going to wait at least a week before I tell him. I'm going to see a doctor Tuesday while we are in Richmond, just to make sure it's real. I want to be totally sure before I scare the heck out of everyone." Skyler informed the group.

"Whatever you decide is fine. Now head on up to the cabin and calm the storm before he freaks out anymore." Eve suggested.

The group went their separate ways. Skyler went back to her condo. Billy and Alex went to the restaurant. Eve went back home, and Allie went to change clothes and go on an afternoon run to clear her head.

Before going into the condo, Skyler sat on the steps and listened to her parents. Fighting as usual and like always, it was about her. Mr. Richardson was having to go out of town next week for a conference, and he wanted to take Skyler with him. He thought she needed to network, and get away from the hoodlums at the resort. "I've had enough of her rebellions Patty. I'm taking her with me." He argued with Skyler's mom. "She's never going to amount to anything if we don't put our foot down. The summer is basically over, and she's already had her fun."

"How dare you talk about my friends?" Skyler busted through the door and screamed at her father without thinking. "You are not taking me anywhere. I'm old enough to make my own decisions."

"Calm down young lady and talk like you have some sense." Mr. Richardson demanded.

"I'm not going to a big college right now. I want to take singing lessons, write songs, and maybe go part time to a community college. I want a job, and I want to take care of myself. I can get an apartment in the city or something.

"You need to let go of those ridiculous dreams." Mr. Richardson stated.

"I'm going to pack my things and I'll be spending the last weeks of summer staying with my friends. I just can't deal with all of this right now." Skyler walked towards her room.

Mr. Richardson shook his head. "Well young lady, you've made your bed. I'll be heading home this weekend, and you'll officially be cut off and on you own. Is that what you want?"

"That's what I need." Skyler stated.

"Okay. Good luck." Mr. Richardson huffed off and went

into the bedroom, slamming the door behind him.

"Mom, please say that you understand. I don't know what I want. I just know what I need, and that's independence." Skyler spoke to her mother.

"Skyler, you need a college education no matter what. Girls don't make it these days without a good foundation to fall back on." Mrs. Richardson advised. "But, I do understand you need to find your place in the world. Just be smart and be safe. I'll add some more money to your savings account. I'm going to head back home after this weekend. Baby just know that you can always come home. Don't pay your father any mind." Patty hugged her daughter. "I'm actually very proud of you. Standing up to him is something that I have always struggled with."

"I'll be fine mom. I've got options. I'm looking forward to the summer ending and embarking on a new adventure." Skyler told Mrs. Richardson that she loved her and went into her bedroom to pack her bags. She would stay with Allie until her parents left for home, then she planned on letting her friends move into the condo for the remainder of the summer. Skyler felt guilty for not telling her mom the truth but she figured that keeping her pregnancy a secret would be for the best.

Once her bags were packed Skyler took her things to Allie's and then went to find Billy. After talking it over they decided to head to Richmond right away. Billy called in sick for work and said he would be going to see his doctor out of town. He told Mr. Davis that he would be back for work Wednesday night. Billy got his pick-up from the employee lot and after telling Allie and Alex their plan the two headed away from the resort and off to Richmond.

CHAPTER NINETEEN

Allie got a phone call from Skyler earlier in the week. She and Billy had called Mr. Davis and they would be staying in Richmond for another week.

It was the following Wednesday when Billy's pick-up finally returned to the resort.

"How did it go?" Allie asked Skyler as she got out of Billy's truck.

"Whose news do you want to hear first?" Skyler asked. The trip to Richmond was definitely a step in the right direction for both of them.

"Just spit it out Skyler!" Allie proclaimed.

"I guess the best way to say it is I now have the perfect job to take care of the three of us." Billy said as he lay he hand on Skyler's stomach.

Allie squealed and jumped up and down with excitement. She was relieved that Billy got the job in Richmond. Now there was a definite plan and less to worry about.

"At least now we know for sure that I am pregnant. And Richmond is different, and big. I think everything is going to work out. I'm relieved and excited." Skyler smiled as she spoke.

"We should celebrate." Alex suggested.

"The condo is free now. You guys ready to move in for the last week of summer." Skyler offered.

"Heck yeah." Alex loved the condo, and he was excited to be able to stay there.

"Oh, before we run into any folks from the resort, there is something I want to let you guys know. It's about Braxton." Allie didn't know how Skyler would feel about the news, but she figured it was better if she heard it from her.

"Is something wrong?" Skyler asked.

"Well, it depends on how you look at it." Alex replied.

"Braxton and Veronica are now a couple. Weird, huh?"

Summer at The Point

Allie informed Skyler.

"Oh well, it's for the best." Skyler was disappointed but it was better this way. "Allie, can I talk to you alone for a second." Allie and Skyler walked away from the truck. "Even if Braxton was the dad, Billy is the better option. It would be best if Braxton didn't even know I was pregnant."

"I agree. Maybe no one else should know. Summer will be over soon, and you won't see any of these people again for another year." Allie wanted the week to be as free from drama as possible.

"Okay girls what's the big secret." Billy called out. He was a little annoyed that Skyler was keeping something from him.

"Nothing sweetheart. We were just talking about the Miss Rock Springs pageant. Allie was a little shy about entering." Skyler lied to cover herself, which led to a smack from Allie.

"I am not entering that contest." Allie whispered in response to Skyler's announcement.

"Oh yes you are. You're taking my place this year. And your going to beat Veronica." Skyler replied back with reassurance.

"You can not be serious." Allie stared at Skyler as she nodded. "And what would my talent be?"

"Aren't you in to the whole poetry and creative writing thing?" Skyler asked.

"Yeah, I write a little poetry." Allie replied. "But that doesn't mean I want anyone to hear it."

"I'm sure you write well. Just recite one of your favorites. It will be a nice change from the normal sing and dance all the others will be doing. Marcy will probably do another tap dance routine. Dull. Veronica will sing of course. You'll be a refreshing change. Now, let's go pick out your evening gown and bathing suit." Skyler was serious. She changed the subject so fast and threw Allie into the contest scene before she really had time to think of an excuse to get out of it.

"Eve said something to me about a gown she had." Allie remembered the conversation they had about the contest.

"I know. I brought it with us the afternoon we stayed with her, and I also have the one I wore last summer. Truth is, Eve signed you up for the contest a while back. Anyway the dresses are in my closet." Skyler smiled.

"Okay, so I guess I have been set up?" Allie didn't really know how she felt about the entire gang arranging for her to compete. They had picked her talent and her dress, and Eve had signed her up. It was all taken care of. "Okay, if it's that important to everyone, I'll do it. The upside is, if I humiliate myself, at least I would only have a week left to face these people. I hope I don't regret this." Allie gave in and decided that it might be fun to dress up and be noticed for once.

In a way, everyone needed this pageant to take their minds off of other stressors that were wearing on them. Skyler needed to be happy with Billy, get over Braxton, and keep the baby a secret. Alex needed to look at future plans. He needed to focus on what he was going to do after graduation. Alex did not want to lose Allie, and he knew he needed to be more serious about life if he wanted to stay with her. Billy had so much on his mind with the move, new job, and baby. He needed a distraction to offer some peace of mind. Allie was scared, not about the pageant, but about what would happen after. She didn't know what life would hand her after leaving the resort. She wanted to keep Alex in her life, but she was worried the distance would tear them apart. Plus, Allie was worried about facing Eric again. She needed the pageant as a reminder that she can do anything she put her mind to. No matter how ridiculous and/or impossible it may seem.

The four spent the next few days trying to sort through their dilemmas while also preparing Allie for her Friday night pageant. Billy and Skyler took long walks early each morning before Billy went in for work, which allowed them to communicate any concerns that may develop from day to day. Billy talked with Mr. Davis, and thanked him for everything. He didn't tell him specifics of his future plans, but he let him know that he had a job waiting for him once the summer ends.

Summer at The Point

Alex spent his spare time avoiding Marcy and John, and trying to figure out how his relationship with Allie was going to survive the distance. Alex would be in his senior year of high school, and Allie would be in her third year of college. It wasn't your typical relationship, but they no longer stressed over that. After lots of discussion, they were able to work out a plan where Allie would come to see Alex every other weekend and when she wasn't coming to Virginia, he would drive down to North Carolina to see her. Everything seemed to be falling in place.

******

The night of the pageant finally came, and Allie was unbelievably nervous. Skyler was backstage helping her dress while Eve, Alex, and Billy watched from the audience. The entire resort was shut down for this pageant so that all female members and employees were eligible to participate. Mr. Davis was the host and the judges were not the ones from the karaoke contest. Instead, the judges were older women from the community who were not affiliated with the resort. There were twenty five contestants. Among them were of course Allie, and also Veronica, Marcy, Katy, and DJ.

All of the girls took the stage in an orderly fashion, presenting themselves first in their evening gowns. Allie was third from last. She looked stunning as she walked out on the stage. She was dressed in a long white gown with sequins that accented her toned figure and olive skin. She came out and took the stage next to Marcy.

Marcy was dressed in a flowing green dress, and Veronica was at the front of the stage in her favorite color, pink. DJ cleaned up nice, and instead of her hair up in her typical tight pony tail, it was down and in long blond ringlets. There were flashy girls, and also those who needed to add a little more make-up. Allie felt like she fell right in the middle, but Alex thought she shined brighter than any other girl up there.

Once all girls were introduced, they returned back stage for costume changes and the talent portion. Mr. Davis told jokes if there were any gaps in the entertainment. All of the girls took the stage one by one showing off their well rehearsed talents. Allie didn't know how well the crowd would appreciate her literary work when all of the others were singing, dancing, or spinning batons. But, Allie had thought long and hard about the poem she would recite. She decided on one that meant a lot to her. She chose the poem she had written for her first year college English class after meeting Jennie Thomas. Jennie was responsible for starting a foundation at a neighboring college that rallied against drunk driving.

"I'm Allie and my talent is somewhat different than the others you have seen tonight. I am going to recite a poem that I wrote titled <u>Wash Away</u>." Allie took a deep breath and began to speak.

"*As the water washes over her, the sadness fades away.*

Summer at The Point

For this moment in time, there is nothing anyone can say.

She brushes her teeth and also her hair,

All while sitting in the same chair.

She wheels herself across the hallway through her bedroom door.

She grabs her clothes out of her broken dresser drawer.

Next, it is off to school to face another day;

And try to hide the hurt she feels from the things that people say.

It was not always like this, everyone used to get along.

But that was before two of her classmates were gone.

Three months ago, Jennie went to a party with her friends;

That was when the tragedy begins.

Everyone was drinking and having fun.

Then Peter and Adam decided their party was done.

It was nearly two in the morning and Jennie's home was not far.

So that is when she and Amy decided to get in Peter's car.

Summer at The Point

Just three stop signs up Peter took a right,

After a left, he took another at the light.

But that was one light too many once it turned red.

Peter never slowed down and in an instant, he and Amy were dead.

Adam was lucky, he just walked away.

But Jennie still cannot walk to this day.

Jennie should have known better; she was top of the class.

But now all she can do is analyze the past.

She hoped with time her classmates would stop the blame.

And no longer associate the fault with her name.

She could have been like Adam and moved away.

Instead, she felt it would be better to stay.

Jennie wheels herself into the auditorium to speak.

She speaks against drunk driving at a different event each week.

Jennie speaks to teens, college students, and adults too.

Summer at The Point

She wants everyone to know that it could even happen to you.

With time, Jennie hopes to be forgiven for her sins.

She needs to receive forgiveness from all of her old friends.

For now she will just head home and to the bathroom she will go;

To wash away her tears and let her prayers flow."

Once she was finished and walked off the stage, Allie felt relieved. The crowd, however, didn't know what to say. Whispers started, but it appeared the general consensus was that everyone appreciated Allie's poetry and the diversity she brought to the competition.

The swimsuit portion of the competition was next, and Allie hoped that the few extra pounds she put on this summer wouldn't be as apparent to the judges as they were to her. She was in line next to the chubby brunette from the neighboring dorm, and Allie felt that might help her chances.

It was two hours before the contest had finally reached an end. Mr. Davis then took the envelope from the judges and called the five finalists to the stage.

Summer at The Point

"Ladies, please come forward as I call your names. Miss Veronica, Miss DJ, Miss Jersey, Miss Deana, and Miss Allie. Audience, let's hear your applause for these fabulous young ladies."

The crowd showed their appreciation as they cheered for their favorites with a standing ovation. "Okay finalists. We will now take votes from our audience. There are two tables at the front of the stage. Guests we would like you to line up and vote for your favorite of our five finalists. The one who receives the most votes will also win a prize tonight. She will be named Fan Favorite and take home $1,000. Our judges will also now decide on their choice for Miss Rock Springs. At this time we will take a thirty minute intermission while we gather your votes and determine our winners. Contestants who are not finalists are eligible to vote. Finalists, please take a seat to the right of the stage. Thank you."

The crowd scattered to cast their votes, and visit the restroom. Allie took a seat alongside DJ and the other finalists as Mr. Davis instructed.

"I can't believe we are finalists." DJ mentioned to Allie.

"I know. We are the only employees to make it this far. Kind of cool, huh." Allie replied.

"Seriously cool. And look at Veronica down there blowing kisses at Braxton. Hope that doesn't influence the outcome. Weird that they are a couple now." DJ commented back.

"Yeah, it is weird. But it looks like you have your own cheering squad out there too." Allie was talking about Mike Carmichael. He had his stare fixated on DJ. DJ smiled as she looked up at him and waived casually.

"Yeah. I have to say things with Mike have turned out a lot better than I thought. I met his parents last weekend, and they seemed to like me okay. So hopefully we'll continue to see each other. What about you and Alex.?" DJ inquired.

"We're doing alright. We are going to stay together and try the long distance thing. I have to say, I never thought I would end up with someone like him, but I'm sure glad I did. I'm crazy about that kid, you know. I'm excited about a future with him." Allie's eyes always seemed to sparkle when she talked about Alex.

The thirty minutes of voting and decision making seemed like an eternity to Allie. She just wanted to be done with it, and enjoy this last week with Alex before she had to go back to school. Allie was scanning the crowd, and for the first time she noticed how sociable Alex was. He had to have talked to fifty different people as he made his way through the crowd of voters. Once Alex noticed Allie was watching him, he walked up as close to her as the judges would allow and said, "You are amazing, I just wanted you to know that." Then he winked at her the same way he did when they first met earlier in the summer. Once he saw

209

the bright smile he was hoping for, Alex went back and took his seat.

The wait was finally over. Mr. Davis came back to the stage, and the crowd began to take their seat. "Okay ladies and gentleman, the last votes are being tallied. Ah, here is the envelope. First I am going to announce the fan favorite. The young lady that wins this will no longer be eligible for the title of Miss Rock Springs. That way everyone has a fair shot." Mr. Davis explained. And this year's fan favorite contestant receiving the $1,000 is..." Mr. Davis draws suspense as he opened the envelope slowly. "You're favorite waitress and mine, Miss Allie Brinkley." Allie was shocked that she had won this award. She stood up to accept her check, and say thank you to the crowd. "Now time to see who's taking home the crown. This year's runner-up Miss DJ Scott." DJ stepped forward to receive a bouquet of flowers. "And this year's Miss Rock Springs is none other than last years champion Miss Veronica Macintosh."

Veronica received her prize and took the microphone to deliver her acceptance speech. "I would like to thank everyone for being here tonight. This is my second Miss Rock Springs crown and I am very appreciative of the nomination; however I feel that I don't deserve it. I just want to take this time to say that I am sorry to the girls who have been hurt by me this summer. I've always been good at pageants and competitions because I'm a good competitor, and I perform well under pressure. But the truth is, outside the competition I've been conniving, deceitful, and ruthless." The crowd watched in amazement as Veronica confessed all of her wrongdoings.

"She really is different." Marcy whispered to Braxton.

"Standing up here tonight and confessing this to everyone is a very hard thing for me to do. I've never been good at admitting when I'm wrong. But I was wrong in so many different situations, and for that I am truly sorry. Allie and Alex, I should never have tested your relationship. To Benita and the other's whose rooms that I broke into, I will return all of your things tonight. What I did was uncalled for. And finally, Skyler Richardson, I just want to say to you that I was jealous of you and all you have. You are an amazing person, and I hope all goes well with you and Billy. And if you have time tomorrow before I leave for home, I want to sit down and really talk to you. I think it would be good for both of us." Veronica was beginning to tear up, so she quickly brought her speech to an end by saying. "Mr. Davis if it is alright with you and the judges, I would like to hand my crown and prize money over to Skyler Richardson. She is the real Miss Rock Springs." Mr. Davis took the crown from Veronica and motioned for Skyler to come to the stage. Skyler was hesitant to stand in front of the crowd, she was shocked that Veronica would do something this selfless. Skyler walked up the side steps and Mr. Davis offered her the microphone at this point.

"Wow." Skyler said as she tried to take in what was

Summer at The Point

happening. "I don't feel I deserve this. I didn't even participate in the pageant, so I don't think it's fair that I take the crown. Veronica, I appreciate your apologies." Skyler smiled back at Veronica. "I think the crown should stay with Veronica. She earned it with her poise, her performance, and her speech. I'm impressed that you could stand up here and do what you just did. You won this contest fair and square." Skyler took the crown and sash from Mr. Davis and placed them on Veronica. "Ladies and Gentlemen, your Rock Springs Queen!" Skyler announced, the crowd rose to applaud even though they were not quite sure what had just happened.

The crowd made their way to the stage to congratulate Veronica and the rest of the contestants. While everyone was celebrating, Skyler snuck off away from stage and back to Billy.

"I wonder what made Veronica give that speech. Someone must have some real dirt on her or something." Skyler suggested.

"I actually respect her for what she did. It really took some guts." Billy gave his opinion to Skyler as he watched the members walk up to the stage to hug the winners.

"Yeah it was pretty cool of her to apologize. I just want to know what made her do it. But that's probably something I'll never know." Skyler replied.

"Very unexpected that is for sure. I think maybe she just had a wake up call and realized her hateful ways weren't getting her anywhere. Plus, she seems to be pretty happy to have a relationship with Braxton. Maybe all she needed was a little love in her life." Billy joked. "Looks like Marcy will be the resort villain now."

"Ha ha, Maybe." Skyler thought about what Billy just said about Veronica and Braxton's so called relationship. She didn't think Veronica needed Braxton. She thought that Braxton needed Veronica. "I wonder what she needs to talk to me about." Skyler thought to herself. She wondered if perhaps it had to do with Braxton? "Hey Miss Fan Favorite!" Skyler announced as Allie and Alex approached her.

"I know, can you believe it?" Allie grinned as she held out her check. "I can definitely use this. Thanks for recruiting voters guys." Allie knew that Alex and Skyler's popularity had something to do with her victory.

"You did really great out there tonight." Skyler complimented.

"Thanks. So can you believe Veronica? Wow! What's gotten into her?" Allie asked.

"Apparently Braxton." Alex stated as he pointed to the happy couple sitting on the front of the stage grinning and greeting members and guests who made their way up to congratulate Veronica.

All four of them chuckled, but inside Skyler felt as if she had lost her best friend, Braxton. She was mad at herself for still caring. If she couldn't convince herself that there were no longer any feelings involved, how could she convince anyone else. Skyler regrouped quickly, and once again reminded herself that her relationship with Billy is all that mattered now.

"Well, I guess we should head on back to the condo." Billy suggested.

"You guys go on back. I'm going to go ahead and talk to Veronica." Skyler remarked.

"Are you sure?" Allie questioned in a surprised manner.

"Yeah. I'll be there shortly. I'm going to pull her away from Braxton now. I'll see ya'll in a little bit." Skyler kissed Billy and walked to meet Veronica at the stage.

"I'm not sure if this is a good idea." Alex mentioned as he grabbed Skyler's hand in passing. After all, Veronica could have faked her apology, and her desire to get to know Skyler.

"It will be fine." Skyler assured Alex.

"Okay. Come on boys let's go." Allie ushered the guys out the door so Skyler could have her alone time with Veronica.

CHAPTER TWENTY

Skyler walked up to the stage where Veronica and Braxton were sitting. "Hey." Skyler spoke shyly.

"Hey." Veronica and Braxton said in sync.

"Braxton can you give us a minute." Veronica asked.

"Sure. I guess." Braxton replied. He hoped Veronica wasn't going to stir anything up. He figured that she was going to confess about the birth control mishap even though they had planned on keeping it from Skyler in the beginning.

Braxton went to find his dad and help with the clean-up. Most of the crowd had left by now, except for a

215

few stragglers still saying there goodbyes. Nearly all of the members would be leaving this Sunday, so for most of them their summer had come to an end. Skyler and Veronica decided to walk out onto the balcony for their talk.

"You might want to sit down." Veronica started the conversation. "And please don't hate me or hurt me after I tell you this."

Skyler was beginning to feel a little uneasy. "Well, you definitely have my full attention now." She sat on the railing. "Okay, go on."

"It was the start of summer, and I had already made up my mind that I wasn't going to let you be the center of attention for another season. I wanted people to see you as unattractive and easy. I wanted the guys to want me for a change. So I went to my mother's clinic and I..." Veronica took a deep breath. "I stole fertility pills and swapped them with your birth control pills. I thought if you got pregnant then the guys would no longer find you as appealing. I thought you would lose Braxton for good. I wanted to mess up your life Skyler, and for that I am so very sorry. I don't think I realized that you really might actually get pregnant. I guess I really didn't think." Veronica confessed as she braced herself for whatever reaction Skyler might have. "Please, I know it's going to take time, but I hope you'll forgive me. What I did was immature and irrational."

"How could you tamper with not only my body, but my

entire world?" Skyler was furious, hurt, and scared all at once. "I don't even know what to say." Skyler turned her back to Veronica and walked toward the side of the balcony.

"I know that no matter what I say, it will not change what I did. I promise I will never do anything like this again to anyone." Veronica stated.

"I would hope not. I'm pregnant Veronica. Do you realize how much of a big deal that is?" Skyler asked.

"I know. I'm sorry." Veronica continued to apologize.

"What do you mean by 'I know'?" Skyler asked.

"Braxton and I figured out you were pregnant." Veronica stammered. "Once he told me how you were feeling, I ended up telling him what I had done."

"Are you serious?" Skyler asked annoyed.

"We had decided not to say anything to anyone, but I had to tell you how it happened. I feel terrible." Veronica responded.

"So Braxton knows. Great!" Skyler remarked sarcastically. "He knows all of this, and you're a couple? It makes no sense."

"He forgives me. He knows that I'm working on becoming a better person." Veronica was desperate for Skyler to forgive her.

Summer at The Point

"I can't think about this right now." Skyler walked away. "I need to find Braxton."

"I understand. I'm just so sorry Skyler." Veronica continued to apologize as Skyler walked away from her.

Skyler went back into the building and found Braxton sweeping confetti up off the stage. "We need to talk." Skyler demanded.

"Okay. Calm down." Braxton knew this was coming. He followed Skyler back out onto the balcony.

"We need a minute." Skyler snapped at Veronica as she held the door open for her to go inside. Once Veronica disappeared behind the closed door Skyler asked Braxton, "is there something you want to ask me or tell me?"

"I didn't know for sure Skyler." Braxton defended himself. "I hoped it wasn't true."

"So I assume you are know what I'm talking about?" Skyler asked.

"You being pregnant." Braxton responded. "I had no part in what Veronica did. I hope you know that."

"I know, she said it was all her. But what's disturbing to me is that you are in a relationship with her crazy butt. What in the world is that really about? Especially after you found out what she had done to me and possibly to us?" Skyler knew that Braxton had to have considered that he might be the father.

"What happened has nothing to do with me. Billy is your guy and nobody is going to question it. This thing we have or had or whatever, it is over for now. I can't be involved when there is an innocent life in the equation. For now, I think it's best for me to lay low." Braxton didn't want to give anyone an inkling that may be involved in Skyler's predicament.

"You know Braxton, I'm glad you have Veronica." Skyler said with a scowl. "You two deserve each other."

"I'll always care for you Skyler. I just am not the settling down type. You said so yourself. And as far as my relationship with Veronica, well it's really none of your business. Everyone deserves to be happy Skyler." Braxton argued back.

"You know, I'm glad I have Billy. He's stable, supportive, and he's crazy about me. What more can I ask for? What happened to you saying you'll always be there?" Skyler questioned as she tried to calm herself.

"I will be, just not quite in the way I was before." Braxton said softly as he patted her shoulder. They never could stay mad at each other for too long.

"Okay, I understand. I just needed to know because, I cannot even begin to imagine a life without you in it." She confessed as she twirled a piece of his hair. She liked it this length. It was not as uncontrollable as the afro he had years back, but it was still long enough for her to run her fingers through.

Braxton looked around to make sure they were alone, then he reached out to grab her hand and kiss her cheek. "I'm here for you Skyler no matter what. And once the baby is born, if you're not happy with Billy, I hope you'll keep me in mind." Braxton remarked playfully.

"Same old Braxton. You can change the exterior, but the interior will always be the same." Skyler smiled shyly.

"Well, you might not like this next part." Braxton cautioned.

"Go on, I want to hear it." Skyler prodded.

"I think for now, we should say our good byes and head our separate ways for a while. You have my number and I have yours, so we should only keep in touch by phone for now." Braxton suggested.

Skyler couldn't believe that this was it. She knew that Braxton was right. These were sensitive times. She needed to really put full effort into her relationship with Billy, for all there sakes. Plus, in just two days Braxton would be leaving to go visit his grandmother in Wilson until school started, and Skyler would be leaving with Billy as well. "You know I'll probably call you everyday."

"I think that will be alright, if that's what you need to

do." Braxton replied.

"I'm actually excited. I think it will be good for me to step out from under my dad's wing. I also need to rely less on you and more on myself." Skyler confessed.

"Did you tell your parents?" Braxton asked concerned.

"Not about the pregnancy, I'm keeping that a secret for a while. It's just that I finally told my dad that I didn't want to go to college in the fall. I told him I needed my independence, and with that he cut me off." Skyler replied. "Surprisingly though, mom said she was proud of me. Go figure."

"I know this isn't the way you wanted your independence, but I'm proud of you for standing up to your dad. You'll be fine without your parents. I just hope you keep singing." Braxton has always loved Skyler's voice. He knew she was gifted, and he hoped she would share her gift with the world.

"The desire for independence is driven by my desire to sing. I want to work fulltime on my songwriting and singing. Billy will be starting a job in Richmond, and I'm moving there with him. I won't be working at first, so I'll be able to do some things for me for a change. It's going to be great." Skyler smiled at Braxton showing him how excited her plans made her.

"Wow, Richmond, really? Definitely different than the small town living I'm used to, but I'm sure you'll love it.

I'm glad we had this chance to talk. I think everything is going to work out just fine." Braxton grabbed her hand once again. "Well, Veronica is probably freaking out right about now. I better get going." Braxton kissed her hand. "Take care. I'll come visit once we agree the time is right."

"Okay, thanks Braxton. Well, go find Veronica. I'm going to head in myself in a little bit. Before you go, just say that you'll miss me." Skyler demanded.

"You know I'll miss you." Braxton winked and then disappeared inside to find Veronica.

Skyler was now all alone out on the balcony. She sat on the bench looking out over the water. She had never thought of herself as the type of girl who would be in this situation. She couldn't believe Veronica did this. Skyler always knew that Veronica was evil, but this time she really crossed the line. She didn't know if she would tell Billy about what Veronica had done. He would probably overreact, and nothing good would come of it. Skyler was pretty nervous about how fast things were changing. She didn't think she would let Billy know that either. She was glad the summer was ending. She knew that if she hung around any longer, it would only a matter of time before everyone found out her secret. Skyler used to like being the topic of conversation, but this time she didn't want to be around when the rumor mill began to churn out new 'did you hears'. This really was it. Her family had pulled away, her first love was with someone else, and now she was going to be a mother. When the summer started Skyler vowed to find excitement and adventure, but she never imagined it would play out like this.

******

It was the Thursday afternoon after the pageant and the employee cabin was slowly clearing out. Everyone was saying there goodbyes, and exchanging numbers and email addresses. DJ wouldn't be taking the bus back home like she originally planned. Instead, Mike would be giving her a ride back to Wilmington. Back at the condo, Allie and Skyler were saying their teary farewells. They both agreed how there friendship was an unexpected surprise that would continue for a lifetime. They promised to visit frequently when their schedules allowed.

"That's the last of it." Billy announced as he slammed the tailgate. "See you around man." Billy shook Alex's hand. "Thanks for everything Allie. Ya'll are welcome to visit any time." Billy hugged Allie as she reminded him she was glad to have helped.

"Good luck on finding a place. Let us know when you do." Alex remarked. "Ya'll are staying a hotel for now, right? Allie did you get the number?"

"Yeah, she's got the number." Skyler answered as she hugged Alex goodbye.

Everyone sighed at the thought of the summer ending.

Summer at The Point

Then Skyler and Billy climbed in his truck, and headed off to their new life. Allie and Alex stayed behind in order to have more time to say farewell. Alex walked to the employee lot to get Allie's car, and park it in front of the condo behind the tanned four-door that he had borrowed from Eve.

"I'll come see you next weekend. If that's okay?" Alex asked as he shut the car door.

"You better." Allie said as she smacked his arm playfully.

"Want me to follow you to the interstate?" Alex offered.

"It's not necessary." Allie answered. "I do need to get going, I guess."

"I know." Alex picked her up and spun her around while he kissed her.

"I'll miss you." Allie said as Alex put her down. "I love you."

"I love you too." Alex replied. "Call me once you get to the highway."

"Okay. I'll see you next weekend then." Allie was sad even though it would not be long before they saw each other again.

They hugged tight one last time and followed each other off the resort. As Allie turned left at the main road,

Summer at The Point

Alex took a right. This was it, the summer had really ended. Allie turned up her radio and sang along, smiling as she remembered that night she saw Alex dancing on the rocks so free spirited and full of life. She then laughed as she recalled the night she first fell in love with his innocence, and she couldn't forget those lovable dimples. Allie was so glad to have had such an unforgettable summer. She could not wait to get back to school and write about the friendship, love, and self-discovery she found at The Point.

IMAGINE... always!

About the Author

Kelly Traylor has always had a strong interest in creative writing. As a child, she enjoyed sitting for hours at a time reading, writing, and imagining. Working as a nurse and continuing to seek higher education has taken time away from writing in the past. However, now she is able to balance all of her loves and begin sharing her stories with others.

www.ingramcontent.com/pod-product-compliance
Lightning Source LLC
Chambersburg PA